"This bed is pretty w P9-EMF-273
murmured. "I think we can manage."

"Uh, sure." Amanda watched him turn off the light. The mattress shifted. He was lying on the edge of the bed. He looked stiff and uncomfortable. But she wasn't going to invite him to get undressed. Yet.

Dear Doctor, she thought. *Is it possible for a man and a woman who are attracted to each other to share the same bed and not end up making love? Signed, Curious and Hot.*

Dear Curious. She answered her own question. *Of course it's possible for a man and a woman who are attracted to each other to be in close proximity and agree not to engage in hanky-panky.*

Hmm. Hanky-panky. A nice old-fashioned term. A wave of heat swept over her body, and she knew she was in trouble.

She'd told him to share the bed with her. Now she had to keep her cool. Just then he shifted uncomfortably and she wondered if he was having the same problem she was. When she found herself staring at his jeans to see if he had an erection, she clamped her teeth together.

She'd sentenced herself to lying next to this sexy man all night long. She was hot, she was needy. And she knew he felt exactly the same.

So what were they going to do about it?

Dear Reader,

Long ago when I wrote mainly nonfiction, I had a job working
with a sexual therapist on an advice column in a national women's
magazine. We'd get together every month, open letters from
readers and decide what to answer. Then she'd dictate notes to
me--which I'd polish up and send to the magazine. I learned a lot
from the experience. For years I've wanted to use that knowledge
in a novel.

Finally I've found the right story—*Bedroom Therapy*. Psychologist
Amanda O'Neal is just starting her career as a sexual advice
columnist. She's not so sure she can handle the job. And she's
got another problem, too. Somebody may be trying to kill her.
But private detective Zachary Grant has vowed to protect her.
Danger and desire throw them into a pressure cooker of
emotions.

The mix makes for one of the hottest novels I've ever written.
And despite the danger hovering in the background, there's
a playful quality to the story that surprised me. I enjoyed every
moment of it. I hope you do, too.

Best,

Ruth Glick, writing as Rebecca York

Books by Rebecca York

BEDROOM THERAPY

Rebecca York

Ruth Glick writing as Rebecca York

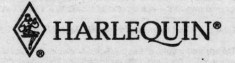

HARLEQUIN®

TORONTO • NEW YORK • LONDON
AMSTERDAM • PARIS • SYDNEY • HAMBURG
STOCKHOLM • ATHENS • TOKYO • MILAN • MADRID
PRAGUE • WARSAW • BUDAPEST • AUCKLAND

ISBN 0-373-79121-6

BEDROOM THERAPY

Ruth Glick writing as Rebecca York.

Copyright © 2004 by Ruth Glick.

This edition published by arrangement with Harlequin Books S.A.

® and TM are trademarks of the publisher. Trademarks indicated with ® are registered in the United States Patent and Trademark Office, the Canadian Trade Marks Office and in other countries.

Visit us at www.eHarlequin.com

Printed in U.S.A.

1

DEAR ESTHER,

I have a problem that I can't talk about with anyone I know. My husband is in the navy and he's on a three-month cruise. Sometimes I get so lonely I don't know what to do. And sometimes I get so hot for him it pushes me over the edge. I mean, I have to make myself come. It feels good when I do it and I always imagine my husband's making love to me. But afterward I feel *so* guilty. What should I do?

Sincerely,

Lonely and Hot in Norfolk

Amanda O'Neal put down the letter she'd been reading and ran a hand through her shoulder-length blond hair. Standing up, she paced over to the window of her office and gazed out at a motorboat speeding up the Choptank River with a man and a woman in it, laughing and enjoying the bright summer afternoon.

A pang of envy shot through her. They were outside on a beautiful Saturday afternoon in early summer, having a good time, and she was cooped up in her little rented house in St. Stephens, reading sexually explicit letters.

She glanced back at the laptop computer on her desk, then down at her pale skin. She could take her laptop out on the patio and get some tan on her legs while she worked.

The prospect was tempting, but she knew in her heart that she'd just be adding one more distraction.

Her gaze flicked to the letter she'd put down. It was one of a stack that the postman had delivered this week—all in plain gray canvas sacks. Should she answer Lonely and Hot in Norfolk or tackle a different question?

She tried a few phrases aloud, thinking about her own father and mother. "Probably your parents drummed it into you that masturbation was evil. Or was it society that taught you it was unhealthy? Not so long ago, they used to tell kids that touching yourself 'down there' would make hair grow on your palms," she said, then grimaced.

Talking to herself was a bad habit she'd gotten into while writing her scholarly papers—reciting key phrases to make sure they didn't sound too stiff.

She glanced back toward the letter lying on her desk. Should she talk about masturbation in the animal kingdom? No, that was going a little too far, she decided. And so was the sentence about hairy hands.

But she was going to be honest and to the point in her answer. She wanted to help that woman who had poured out her heart to Esther Scott.

Of course, there really was nobody named Esther Scott, the woman whose pseudonym appeared at the top of the widely read sexual advice column in *Va-*

nessa, one of the country's leading women's magazines. There'd never been a real Esther Scott.

Until last month, the much-talked-about column had been written by a distinguished sexual therapist named Esther Knight. Because she had wanted to keep the identity of her patients confidential, she had picked a pen name when she'd started writing articles and then the column.

Unfortunately, Esther was dead, the victim of a hit-and-run accident. The editor of *Vanessa,* Beth Cantro, was an old college friend of Amanda's. And when she'd needed a fast replacement to author the column that received hundreds of letters each month, she'd turned to Amanda.

"But I see *Vanessa* on every newsstand," Amanda had protested. "Women from their early twenties to their fifties read your magazine. You've got a reputation to uphold. How can you use somebody who's never done this before?"

"Well, because we do have that reputation—now. When Vanessa Summers put two million of her personal fortune into the first issue, she didn't know it was going to be such a hit. But we've got the right mix of sex, fashion, food, entertainment, sex, decorating, hair and makeup advice, the diet of the month, sex, meaty articles on women's issues, sex, relationships."

Amanda had laughed. "Okay, I get the picture."

"I know how you feel, actually," Beth admitted. "When Vanessa retired to her Montana ranch with her new husband and picked me to replace her, I felt like I couldn't fill her shoes. But I found out I have excellent editorial judgment. You can do it, I'm positive. Basically, this job just requires the same skills you've learned teaching your graduate seminars in human sexuality,'' Beth had argued.

"It's a lot more public forum than a graduate seminar. What's the circulation of your magazine?''

"A couple million.''

Amanda groaned.

"I'm not trying to scare you off. I'm trying to convince you that taking the job makes sense. It will be good practice for that book you keep telling me you want to write. You worked for Esther when you were a graduate student. That gives you a leg up. And I want a Ph.D. for this job—to give the answers authority.''

"Yeah. Right,'' Amanda muttered aloud as she began pacing again back across the office then plopped down in the desk chair.

During an afternoon of arm-twisting and wine coolers on the patio, she'd accepted Beth's offer—partly because she was on a leave of absence from the psychology department of Harmons College, and she couldn't use the excuse of a full teaching schedule. Plus, the money was excellent.

Now the deadline for her first column was looming, and she wondered if she'd been crazy to take the job.

Flexing her fingers, she poised them over the computer keyboard. The trouble was, giving sexual advice was such a big responsibility. But she knew her subject, she thought as she opened a file and started typing. And she knew how to make women feel good about themselves and their sexuality. At least, that had been true of her students.

Dear Lonely and Hot,

Stop feeling guilty. Masturbation is a perfectly normal sexual outlet. You love your husband; but he's away, and there's nothing wrong with taking care of your sexual needs. Whenever a woman is without a partner, self-pleasuring is an excellent alternative to making love with a man. And, plus, it's a good way for a woman to learn more about her own sexual responses. If she finds out what she likes when she's alone, she can better express her likes and dislikes to her sexual partner.

She leaned back, reading over what she'd written, moving restlessly in the chair as she considered her advice.

Was it a little warmer in the room?

She pulled at the neck of her T-shirt as she considered the letter and her reply. The woman in Norfolk was married. Should she add something for single women—who might feel guilty about taking care of their own needs? Should she also point out that masturbation was really the only kind of safe sex?

Probably that was going too far. But maybe she could find a letter from a single woman who had asked a question about pleasuring herself, and make masturbation the topic of the column.

She'd already opened a bunch of envelopes. They'd been sent to her in a U. S. Postal bag, directly from the *Vanessa* mail room. Had there been another one on the subject? She couldn't remember.

Ignoring the annoyingly full feeling in her breasts,

she began shuffling through the letters, looking for another one to include.

After going through twenty-five letters, Amanda still hadn't found one. There were hundreds more, some unopened and left over from Esther's tenure. But reading them all was going to take a lot of time.

Could she just write another masturbation question herself? She was a single woman. It had been a long time since she'd been with a man. Not since Bob Burns.

She repressed a small shudder. Bob was the new man in the psych department at Harmons. Which was one of the reasons why she was taking a leave of absence.

Getting mixed up with him had been a big mistake. The trouble was, she'd thought he was a nice guy, and it had turned out that he was envious of her position in the department, so envious that he'd gone to the chairman with tales about her that weren't true.

But lord, at the beginning, he'd been a good lover. She closed her eyes for a moment, remembering the man's practiced sensual touch. He knew how to tease and tantalize and build anticipation—and then deliver what he'd promised—a mind-blowing orgasm.

She hadn't made love with him in nine months. She hadn't been with any man, actually. She'd had the opportunity, of course. But she was being more cautious about relationships.

But that didn't mean she had to give up sexual pleasure. Eyes closed, she reached up with one hand and stroked the side of her breast. When she felt her nipple bead, she used her thumb to find the edge and stroke it lightly through her T-shirt. She wasn't wearing a bra. She never did around the house.

When she realized what she was doing, she lowered her hand and squeezed it into a fist. Bob Burns was the last man on earth she wanted to think about when she was turned on. And besides, she was supposed to be working. She had a deadline, she thought as she rocked back in her seat. The movement sent a little jolt of heat to the lower part of her body.

Damn, this was a heck of a job. And at the moment she was having trouble focusing on what she was supposed to be doing. At least she wasn't sitting in one of the cubicles in *Vanessa*'s plush New York offices pretending to be working. When she'd visited, Beth and her fifty staffers—mostly women but a few men—had been in an uproar, getting ready for the next issue of the magazine. And she'd watched writers and copy editors and art department personnel scurrying around—conferring with each other and getting Beth's final approval on various articles and page layouts.

Better that she was down here. Where nobody could see her slogging through the humiliation of not being able to put two coherent sentences together.

With her teeth clamped together, she reached toward the pile of correspondence again just as the phone rang. The caller ID told her it was Beth, of all people.

She waited through four rings, until the answering machine picked up.

"This is Amanda O'Neal. I'm not here to take your call right now. So please leave a message."

"Amanda. Amanda." Beth's voice came at her

several levels too high. "If you're there, Amanda, pick up."

She flexed her fingers, but kept them away from the phone. She'd been thinking about Beth, and here she was on the phone!

"I'd like to see what you've written on your first column, to make sure you're on the right track."

Amanda groaned. Sometimes she'd thought that Esther's answers weren't... She searched for the right words and settled on professional enough. Now that she was sitting in the dead woman's seat, she was finding it wasn't all that easy. She had one letter and one response, but she wasn't going to tell her friend that was all she'd accomplished—which meant that she wasn't going to answer the phone.

"And I'd better warn you about Zachary Grant. Well, not a warning, actually. He's coming to interview you. He's a real dish. Dark hair. Dark eyes. Tanned skin. Sensual lips. A blade of a nose. Thick, sooty lashes. Think black Irish. He looks like a mountain climber or something. He's perfect for you. Or I wouldn't have given him your address."

Amanda swore under her breath. A stud muffin mountain climber. Just what she needed. Beth wasn't supposed to give her address or phone number to *anyone*. And now she was sending a reporter? She reached for the phone to ask what was going on, just as Beth's tone changed.

"Oops—got to go. Editorial crisis. I'll get back to you later."

By the time Amanda got the receiver to her ear, she was listening to dead air.

Great! Beth was sending her some guy who was

perfect for her. Like *she'd* know, when Amanda didn't even know herself.

ZACHARY GRANT pulled his car onto a side road hemmed in by cattails on one side and a lazy-looking river on the other. After cutting the engine, he put away the computer directions that he'd been following. He was always very methodical about his work. And now that he was right around the corner from Amanda O'Neal's house, he wanted to check his notes before ringing her doorbell.

He'd driven down from New Jersey early that morning, his mission to talk to the woman who was now writing the sexual advice column in *Vanessa*.

She was a far cry from Esther Knight, a woman he'd never heard of until a few days ago. She'd been an old bat in her late sixties. But she'd written some sexual stuff that would curl your hair. Her career of telling people what to do with their private lives had been cut short by a hit-and-run accident—an accident that the family believed was murder.

He blew out a breath, pushed back the seat, and stretched out his long legs. Then he flipped through the folder with his notes and the material he'd collected. First he reviewed what he knew about Esther Knight. Then he got out his notes from Beth Cantro, *Vanessa*'s editor.

One thing he'd picked up on was that Cantro seemed pretty protective of Amanda O'Neal. When he'd talked to her on the phone, she'd been reluctant to give him the new advice columnist's address. She'd insisted that he come to her office, where she'd grilled him as though she were the woman's marriage broker, not her editor.

Really, what did it matter that he was thirty-two, single and well established in his chosen profession?

But he'd dutifully given her the information—then run a background check on Dr. O'Neal. She'd gotten herself in a bit of trouble at Harmons College. From what he could gather, it looked like they weren't going to give her tenure. Which meant that she needed this job.

He shuffled through the folder and found her photograph. According to her bio, she was thirty-one. Although she was blond and blue-eyed, with a heart-shaped face and nicely curved lips, nobody would ever mistake her for a dumb blonde. The way she looked out at the camera conveyed a kind of no-nonsense approach to life.

He picked up a copy of *Vanessa* that Beth Cantro had given him and turned to the sexual advice column. Amanda O'Neal's work hadn't appeared yet—so he assumed these letters and answers were from the Esther Knight era.

My boyfriend and I get along pretty well. We've been together for six months, and he's asked me to move in with him. But one thing worries me. His penis is small. Does that make a difference in our sexual relationship?

He grimaced, wondering how the chick who had voiced the complaint would rate *his* cock. He'd always thought he was pretty average in that department. Well, maybe a bit above average. But were there women who only wanted guys who looked like stallions?

Esther Knight's answer began with a sentence he didn't much like. "A big penis is a turn-on to a lot of women." He skimmed the rest, put off by the tone of Dr. Knight's answer. Really, he was more comfortable with the man-to-man advice in the *Playboy Advisor*.

Would Amanda O'Neal be as flip in her responses as the dead woman? Again, he looked at her publicity photo. It was easy to imagine her as a prude. But would the magazine hire someone who would seriously alter the tone of the column? If they did, wouldn't readers notice?

He opened another magazine. And another letter caught his eye.

Dear Esther,

My boyfriend and I keep having the same argument about what we do when we're making love. He wants me to do oral sex on him. But he hates doing it to me. So I feel like I'm getting—um—the short end of the stick.

Selfish bastard, he thought, without checking out Esther's words of wisdom. Really, reading this right now was a mistake. He wanted to be calm, cool and collected when he met Ms. O'Neal. And reading these letters was making him anything but. How did O'Neal deal with this on a daily basis?

Either she had to be a cold fish, or she must be in

a constant state of arousal. It would be amusing to
find out which.

And maybe she'd like to help him with the little
problem he'd been having since his divorce.

Yeah, sure! No way was he going to talk to her
about anything intimate.

He sighed. Too bad he couldn't step into a cold
shower before the interview. Or take a quick dip in
the river.

Unbuckling his seat belt, he heaved himself out of
the car and turned toward the shoreline. A little breeze
was blowing—enough to cool him off a couple of
degrees. He walked across the street, staring out at
the water. A white van was parked not far away. Apparently the people inside wanted their privacy, because as he walked toward the vehicle, the engine
started and the van pulled off the shoulder of the road,
the tires throwing up a shower of gravel as it sped
away.

He looked after it, his nose for trouble twitching.
He'd walked casually across the street, and the vehicle's driver had immediately left. Either that was a
big coincidence, or—

Or what?

Had he disturbed a drug deal—or something else?

He glanced toward the corner. From where he was
standing he could see the O'Neal house. So was
somebody staking her out? He'd like to know.

AMANDA STARED at the phone. Beth was going to call
again, and she couldn't keep ducking her. She went
back to the stack of letters so she'd have something
to report besides one letter answered.

Maybe she couldn't make self-pleasuring the topic.
Maybe she should go with a mix of questions.
There were so many.

Dear Esther,
I have a new boyfriend. He's a lot more into
foreplay than the last guy I went with. Anyway,
last night we were fooling around. He started
stimulating my breasts, and all of a sudden, I had
an orgasm. I mean, all he was doing was kissing
me and playing with my nipples and I went off
like a firecracker. Is that normal?
                                        Embarrassed in Ohio

Amanda shifted her shoulders, her own nipples
now painfully tight.

Damn. Maybe she should take a tranquilizer before
she opened any more letters. The assignment would
get easier, she told herself. It *had* to get easier. It
would be like the summer she'd taken a job scooping
ice cream at the Big Dipper. The employees could
have all they wanted. At first she'd gobbled up a lot
of Raspberries & Cream and Chocolate Mint Chip on
her break.

But after a few weeks of gorging herself, dipping
up ice cream had become as exciting as dipping up
barbecued beans. Hopefully, this overdose of sex
would turn out the same way.

She went back to the letter she'd just read, gripping
her lower lip between her teeth as she tried to frame
an answer. Why did women get defensive so easily?
Why did they always think something was wrong
with them? Really, the lady with the sensitive breasts
was lucky. She had a guy who wanted to turn her on.
She was highly sensual.

Dear Embarrassed in Ohio,
There's nothing wrong with you. Be glad that you are so sexually responsive. Lots of women would envy you. There are all kinds of ways for a female to reach orgasm. Some women feel that there's something wrong with them if they don't climax during intercourse. But each one of us needs to experiment to find out how she responds best.

She stopped, arching her back as she moved her bottom in the seat. How far should she go here? Should she go over all the ways a woman could reach climax? Maybe she should look at some of Esther's old columns to see how much she expanded on each topic.

She got up and went to the bookcase where she'd stored several notebooks that Beth had given her. In them were ten years of Esther's sexual advice columns.

Instead of staying in the living room, she carried the books to the bedroom where she could spread them out. Climbing on the bed, she picked up one of the books and began thumbing through the pages.

Two years ago, a woman had asked if bondage was a normal part of a sexual relationship.

Esther had answered:

"If both partners are interested in trying bondage games, there's nothing wrong with experimenting in this area. But one partner should never force the other. And if one partner keeps pushing the subject when the other is turned off by it, you should wonder why he or she is making it so important."

Bondage. That was a little extreme she thought, circling one wrist with her thumb and forefinger. On the other hand, there was something very sexy about putting yourself into another person's power. Of course, it had to be someone you trusted implicitly. Because if you picked the wrong guy, you could get into serious trouble.

There was nobody she'd met who she trusted that much, so she'd never played bondage games. Actually there were a lot of things she'd never done.

But it was interesting to think about them. Actually it could be quite sexy with a very special man.

She piled the books on one side of the bed and lay back against the pillows, getting comfortable.

She'd been working hard. There was no reason she couldn't take a break.

She closed her eyes, imagining a man beside her on the bed instead of a pile of notebooks.

What man? Somebody great-looking. With a great body. Clever hands. A man who was as interested in pleasing his partner as in pleasing himself.

She wanted to give him a face, and Beth's description of Zachary Grant came back to her. Dark hair. Dark eyes. Thick, sooty lashes. Tanned skin. Very sensual lips. A blade of a nose. A guy with the physique of a mountain climber or something.

That was all Beth had seen. But what about his penis? What was that like? Considering that question raised her temperature a few notches.

She'd pretended she wasn't interested when Beth had gone on and on about his virtues over the phone. Now that she was alone in her bedroom, she had to admit he had sounded yummy.

And since she was in charge of her own fantasies, she could make him into anything she wanted. He'd be an excellent lover. That was her most important requirement, not the size of his equipment, she decided, as she let her hands hover teasingly over her breasts, then lowered them to brush the hardened tips.

A jolt of sensation went through her. Nice. That was nice. She knew what she liked, knew how to give herself maximum pleasure. She brought her hands lower, lifting her breasts, kneading them gently before letting herself return to the centers.

Her breath was coming in little bursts as she pulled up her T-shirt and repeated the caresses she'd enjoyed earlier—this time on her naked skin.

She'd never climaxed just by breast stimulation, but she got pretty hot that way.

It took only a few moments before she was opening the drawer next to her bed and bringing out her vibrator.

Laying it beside her on the bed, she skimmed her shorts and panties down her legs and kicked them off.

She had just turned on the vibrator when the doorbell rang.

She jumped—startled by the sudden interruption. She was almost naked—her shorts and panties at the end of the bed, her T-shirt pulled up to her neck.

"Go away," she whispered.

The doorbell rang again, and she ignored it. But the mood was broken, and she switched off the vibrator. She'd been enjoying herself in a very adult activity. Now she felt like a little girl caught doing something naughty.

Several seconds passed, and she figured whoever it

was had gone away. Next to her, the phone on the bedside table jangled, and her nerves were so frayed that she snatched it up and shouted, "Yes? Who is it?"

"This is Zachary Grant."

When she didn't answer, he said, "I think Beth Cantro told you about me."

She grimaced. Not him of all people. Not *now*. "Yes, she said you wanted to do an interview. But I'm not—"

He interrupted before she could finish the sentence. "That's okay. I'm right outside your house. You didn't answer the door, but your car is in the driveway, so I decided to give you a call. I'd like to come in and talk to you."

God no, was all she could think, feeling her face flame as she pictured him standing on her doorstep like a mountain climber ready to tackle Mt. McKinley.

What she said was, "I'm not dressed. Give me a minute."

"Sure."

Why had she told him that?

Slamming down the phone, she reached for the shorts and panties she'd discarded on the end of the bed. Quickly she pulled them on, then ran to her closet and took down the bra hanging over one of the clothing hooks. With her T-shirt still around her neck, she shoved her arms into the bra straps and hooked the clasp in back. Then she ran into the bathroom and splashed cold water on her face.

Daring to lift her gaze, she looked into the mirror.

Her face was still flushed and her eyes were bright. What the hell was he going to think she'd been doing?

Well, that was none of his business.

She ran her brush quickly through her hair, then she started back through the bedroom. When she glanced toward the bed, she saw her vibrator lying in the center of the spread.

With a groan, she shoved it under the pillows. Then she stood in the middle of the room, taking several deep breaths before she marched down the hall toward the front door.

2

AMANDA PEEKED through the peephole in the door. Distorted by the fish-eye lense, Mr. Grant had dark hair and dark eyes, a big nose and a long chin.

Steeling herself, she flung the door open, then blinked. The guy standing on the porch looked a lot like Beth had described him. The dark hair was just a little long around the edges, but the shaggy look suited him. The dark eyes were framed by sooty lashes.

"Amanda O'Neal?" he asked.

"Yes."

"Zachary Grant."

From the far side of the threshold, he was staring at her with such intensity that she felt her cheeks go hot, and she had to stifle the impulse to look down and make sure she really was wearing a bra.

Lord, there was no way he could figure out what she'd been doing a few minutes ago. But it sure felt like he'd caught her about to dip her hand into the cookie jar.

He gestured toward the interior of the little house. "Can I come in?"

She wanted to say "no." But Beth was expecting her to talk to this guy. Probably she wanted some publicity for the magazine, although, come to think of it, Amanda wasn't sure how that was going to work, since the real identity of Esther Scott had always been a secret. So what was she supposed to do, give details of her background and attribute them to Esther? Well, she guessed she'd find out.

She stepped aside and gestured toward the living room, then took the opportunity to study him from the back as he walked down the short hall. He was informally dressed in chinos and a dark polo shirt that did a great job of showing off his broad shoulders and beautifully muscled, tanned arms. And the slacks curved seductively around his nice, tight butt.

Which she shouldn't be staring at, she told herself. His physical attributes were nothing to her.

ZACH STOOD looking around the living room, keeping his back to Ms. O'Neal. No, he'd better remember it was Dr. O'Neal. He'd met a lot of Ph.D.'s who were touchy about the title, and he didn't want to set up a confrontational situation.

Of course she didn't look like a doctor—or much like the picture her editor had given him, for that matter.

In her tight little shorts and T-shirt, she seemed much younger. More like a graduate student than a professor.

And she seemed a lot more vulnerable than the woman in that picture. Prettier, actually. And several degrees more nervous.

He'd had a good deal of training in reading people, and his instincts were excellent. From the moment she'd opened the door, he would have said she was being evasive. Was she into something illegal? Or was she just uptight about being in the house alone with a guy she had just met? Some women were like that, he knew. But she hadn't asked to see his identification. Probably because her editor had vouched for him, so to speak.

Which was good, because his own nerves weren't too steady at the moment. He usually sensed within a few minutes how to approach an interview. He was good at putting people at ease and then getting them to spill stuff that they had planned to keep to themselves. Over the years, he'd developed a number of roles that he played during a question and answer session.

He could be Joe Friday from that old television series. Just the facts, ma'am. He could be kindly old uncle Zach who was on your side—until you told him that you'd murdered grandma and dumped her in the river. He could be the naive, unsure kid who'd bumbled into a detective assignment and needed the person he was interviewing to help him out.

He was feeling unsure now. In fact, he didn't know how to play this interview at all. Maybe because it was intimidating questioning a woman who knew so much about sex. And a woman who attracted him—all rolled into one.

Really, how many guys would be comfortable dating a lady who knew how long foreplay was supposed to last and who knew what technique was best on the clitoris?

He was really sorry that thought had jumped into his head because it made it tough for him to turn and look her in the face. Instead, he kept glancing around the room. Dr. O'Neal had only been in this house for a few weeks. In fact, he knew she'd rented it furnished. Yet she'd made it her own.

He could tell she was a professor. The bookshelf

was crammed with big volumes that looked like they came from a university library. All neatly arranged. Probably in alphabetical order by the author. Or maybe she used the Dewey decimal system.

Despite the fact that she had taken over a corner of the living room as an office, the space wasn't all business. There were lots of individual touches that hinted at a very interesting and varied background.

Like, for example, she was either well traveled or she'd spent a lot of time at import shops. Several decorative Spanish-looking plates were propped on the mantelpiece, along with a family of eight-inch-tall dolls that had likely come from Latin America. The beige fabric of the sofa was enlivened with a brightly woven throw. A figure that looked suspiciously like a fertility god sat on the coffee table.

Not your usual art object. The thing was only six inches tall, but it appeared to have a two-inch penis.

As he gazed at that ceramic penis, he was thinking he'd never started off an interview feeling more off balance. Casting around for somewhere else to rest his eyes, he turned to the desk where her laptop computer sat next to a pile of letters. It looked like a lot of people were writing to Esther Scott for advice.

"I guess you were working," he observed.

"Yes," she answered, her voice very thin, and he had to wonder again why she was so nervous. Was there something in that pile of letters she didn't want him to see? Something personal?

The top one was on blue stationery with a wavy edge. Unable to stop himself, he walked over and picked it up, then read the rounded, feminine hand-writing.

My boyfriend says that making love with me is no fun. He says that my vagina is so big that he might as well wave his penis out the window as put it inside me. I don't want to lose him. Is there something I can do to make myself tighter.

"Jesus!" he said aloud.

She'd been standing in back of him where he couldn't see her. Now she came charging across the room like he was about to pocket the damn letter. Before he could take a breath, she snatched it out of his hand.

Looking down at the words on the page, she slid her thumb over the signature. "That's confidential! You can't just go around reading what people have written to Esther."

It didn't matter to him who had written the letter, as long as it wasn't to Dr. O'Neal personally. However, he came up with, "Sorry. But that woman's boyfriend sounds like a jerk."

"Yes."

She stepped around him and laid the paper face-down on the stack.

He should probably drop the subject, but he found himself asking, "Is there something she can do about her physical problem?"

"The Kegel exercises. The same exercises that are used for incontinence. They'll tighten her vaginal muscles if she does them regularly."

"And if the exercises don't work?"

"She might need surgery. Or a guy with a bigger penis." The last part was uttered almost under her breath. But he heard it.

"You think penis size has something to do with it?"

"It could. I don't know the woman or her boyfriend."

Yeah, and what would you do if you met him, ask him to drop his pants? Instead of coming out with that sarcastic comment, he asked, "Then how can you answer her question?"

She sailed into her reply. "I have to try and write a response that will be helpful to that particular reader and also to other readers."

"Like how?"

"I've looked back at Esther's columns. One thing she's tried to get across is that sex should be in the context of a relationship."

"Oh. And what are you trying to get across?"

"Well, the message about relationships is important. I also want to help people feel comfortable with their own sexuality."

Right, he thought. Suppose he told her the problem he'd been having for the past year. Could she make him feel comfortable about that? Yeah, sure.

"Sorry, I didn't mean to lecture," she said, breaking into his thoughts.

"No. I mean, that's okay. It's interesting," he managed to say, thinking that he was probably having the most sexually explicit conversation he'd had since his marriage had crashed and burned. Maybe the most sexually explicit ever. He'd never been good at talking about what went on behind closed bedroom doors, although he'd always thought he was pretty good at doing it. Until recently, anyway.

As long as he could say just about anything he

wanted to a woman who didn't mind giving answers, he asked, "Can you give me an example?"

She thought for a moment. "Well, a common...circumstance with women is that they can't climax during intercourse. They need more direct stimulation. That's likely to make them feel like they're doing it wrong. I want them to know that's perfectly all right."

He found that information startling. And pretty close to home. For a fantasy moment he thought about asking her what she thought about a man who couldn't climax during intercourse. Was that okay, too? And exactly how many men suffered from the problem? And what could they do about it? Before he blurted out something too revealing, he suppressed the questions. He wasn't here to get personal sexual advice.

So he changed the direction of the interview. "How do you get to be a sex therapist?"

It looked like the question had hit a nerve. She squared her shoulders. "I'm not strictly a sex therapist."

"What are you?"

"A psychologist."

"So how did you get this job?" he asked, although he already knew the answer to the question. He simply wanted to find out how honest she would be.

"I guess it's a case of being in the right place at the right time. Beth Cantro, the editor of *Vanessa,* is a friend of mine. She knew I was on leave from Harmons College, and she asked me to take the column after Esther died."

"And you feel qualified to give out sexual advice?"

He knew he'd made the question sound confrontational when he saw her place her fisted hands on her hips. "Of course I'm qualified! I have a Ph.D. in psychology. My area of specialty is human sexuality. And my reading in the field is wide-ranging."

Her complexion had taken on a rosy hue, and he liked the effect. He wanted to ask her how much personal experience she had with the subject—or if she'd gone in for any interesting research of the Masters and Johnson variety. Like every other kid he knew, he'd thumbed through their books in the library stacks. He'd been very interested to find out that they'd had people come into their laboratories, stuck electrodes all over their bodies and then watched them perform sex.

Ever done anything like that, Dr. O'Neal, he wondered. He decided it was prudent to keep that question to himself. And prudent to stop focusing on his own reactions to the woman and the situation.

One thing he knew from her answer; she wasn't entirely confident in the role of Esther Scott, sexual advice columnist. Was that why she was nervous? Was she afraid that he'd challenge her authority?

"Are you expecting to keep this job permanently?" he asked.

"I don't know yet."

"Were you personally acquainted with Esther Knight?"

"Yes. I was her graduate assistant when I was working on my Ph.D. But do you really need to know that kind of stuff to write a magazine article?"

A magazine article. That's what she thought he was doing here? Hadn't Beth Cantro explained it?

Probably he should set Dr. O'Neal straight. But not

yet. The editor had given him too good an opportunity to get information he might not acquire if the good doctor realized why he was here.

"I try to get as much material as I can," he said. "I never know what I'm going to use."

She answered with a tight nod.

"Why don't we sit down," he said, hoping that both of them could relax a little bit.

"How long are you going to be here?" she asked.

"It depends."

She crossed to the wingback chair and sat down stiffly, making sure there was no chance he could sit beside her.

With a shrug, he took the sofa.

"So, did you get this throw in Latin America?" he asked, fingering the bright fabric.

"Ecuador. I spent one summer doing research with Indians in the Andes."

"Related to uh...your area of expertise?"

"No. That was when I was researching my Master's thesis. I was writing about the culture of work in that country—how quickly children were expected to assume adult responsibilities in the family."

"And?"

"On market day, there were eight-year-old girls who walked around with their baby brothers or sisters strapped to their backs while their mothers sold fried bananas from street carts."

He was thinking about how to turn the conversation back to Esther Knight. He leaned back against the cushions, crossed one leg over the other in an attempt to look comfortable, and fished in his pocket for his notebook. Flipping it open to a blank page that he

knew she couldn't see, he pretended to study the blue
lines.

"So, how did you go from the Andes to sexual
research?" he asked.

"I don't do sexual research."

The word research had just slipped out. "Um,
right," he answered. "I meant—what did you call
your field—human sexuality?"

"Yes."

"And how did you end up working for Esther
Knight?"

"When I entered the Ph.D. program, Esther asked
if I wanted to work for her. She suggested that I help
her with a paper she was writing on teenage girls. She
was doing interviews, trying to quantify the reasons
why girls gave in to pressure from their boyfriends to
have sexual intercourse."

Suddenly, he could remember being a horny teenage boy anxious to get his girlfriend to go all the way.
It hadn't been one of the most noble episodes of his
life, as he recalled. Stifling the impulse to run his
finger around the inside of his collar he asked,
"And?"

"If you're really interested in the details, I can give
you a copy of the paper. It was published in the *Jour-
nal of Applied Human Sexuality*."

Applied Human Sexuality. He wasn't going to ask
what else they published. "No. That's all right," he
answered, shifting uncomfortably in his seat. He was
feeling more on edge than he had when he'd walked
in the door. Physically as well as emotionally.

Somehow he didn't seem to be able to get off the
topic of sex. Probably because he was fascinated by
the frank answers Dr. O'Neal was giving. And fas-

cinated with the woman herself. Her dewy good looks and no-nonsense answers made an interesting combination. One that he'd like to explore more fully.

He canceled that thought immediately. He wasn't here to get to know her. He was here because he had a job to do. To introduce a little distance from her, he asked, "Do you mind if I use your bathroom?"

"Not at all."

Glad to escape, he stood up.

"It's through the bedroom. Down the hall."

"Thanks." He made a quick exit, thinking that it would be a good idea if he finished his assignment here as quickly as possible. But leaving the room gave him an opportunity he couldn't pass up.

When he reached the bedroom, he glanced over his shoulder. He couldn't see Dr. O'Neal from the doorway. Perhaps he could get away with a little snooping. If he were here on a social visit, he would have felt guilty about invading her privacy. Actually, he still felt an unsettling twinge as he opened a dresser drawer and looked down at a very nice selection of ladies' lingerie. Then he sternly reminded himself that he was here for a very specific purpose.

So he felt around under her silky panties and bras, then opened another drawer and reached under a pile of neatly folded sweaters. He didn't know exactly what he was looking for, of course. He just knew that people tended to hide incriminating evidence among their personal belongings.

AMANDA WATCHED Zachary Grant's broad shoulders disappear down the hall. He was personable and intelligent, and Beth was right. Under other circumstances, she might have been attracted to him.

No, that was a lie, and she made it a rule never to lie. Especially to herself. She *was* attracted to him. She liked his looks, and she'd actually liked a large part of the conversation. There weren't too many man who were comfortable talking about sex. But Mr. Grant had held his own in the discussion.

Held his own. She couldn't hold back a grin at her unfortunate choice of words. That wasn't what she'd meant, of course. He'd kept his hands where she could see them at all times.

As soon as he stepped into the bedroom, she took the opportunity to cross to the desk and shove the pile of letters into a folder. Nobody else should be looking at them. But no harm had been done really. He wasn't going to put the letter writers' names in his article. Was he? Of course not.

And he wasn't going to quote the letter—was he?

She thought about the wording. Talking about a guy's waving his penis out the window was a pretty distinctive way for a man to express his dissatisfaction. And the woman who had written the letter would surely recognize it.

When Mr. Grant came back, she'd better make the ground rules clear. Anything a reader had written to Esther was off limits.

She was remembering now that the press sometimes sneaked in tidbits the subject of the article wasn't going to appreciate. Like writing, "You'll be interested to know that Miss Movie Star told me not to write anything about her facelift." Yeah, right. Thanks a lot.

She looked down the hall, listened for the sound of the toilet flushing. Had he fallen in? Ordinarily she'd give him his privacy. But he'd had to walk through her bedroom, and suddenly she'd remembered that she'd left her vibrator on the bed.

Although she'd shoved it under the pillow, she hoped to hell she hadn't left part of it sticking out. But she'd been in a hurry. And besides, she hadn't pictured anyone walking into her bedroom.

Sudden concern had her hurrying down the hall. When she reached the doorway, she stopped short, hardly able to believe what she was seeing.

3

Amanda...

"JUST WHAT THE HELL do you think you're doing?"
Amanda demanded, her gaze shooting daggers. He
had absolutely no right to be pawing through her personal stuff, yet there he was, big as life.

At least when Zachary Grant whirled to face her,
she saw embarrassment spreading across his face.

"What are you doing?"

"Investigating a murder."

The matter-of-fact answer went right by her. She
was too focused on her own outrage. In back of him,
her junk drawer stood open. The drawer where she
shoved all kinds of things she didn't know what to
do with. Even in the short time she'd been in St.
Stephens, a lot had accumulated—like grocery store
coupons, the tube of cream she'd gotten in case she
came down with another yeast infection, some credit
cards she had stopped carrying in her wallet.

"Get out of here!" she shouted.

"Sorry," he muttered, shoving his hands deep into
his pockets and looking like a little kid who'd been
caught with a porn magazine.

But he wasn't a little kid. He was a man—who
could be dangerous, she realized belatedly.

"Sorry doesn't cut it," she answered, struggling to
keep her voice from quivering. Probably she should

leave well enough alone, but she heard herself asking, "What are you, some kind of pervert or something?"

He gave her a long look, a look that made her want to take a step back. But she held her ground.

"No," he answered, his voice low and measured. "I'm a private detective. Like I said, I'm investigating a murder."

Now that she'd finally focused on what he was saying, it was the last thing she'd expected to hear. "But...but...you said you were a reporter," she stammered, wondering how she'd gotten it all wrong.

"No, you said it."

She thought about how she'd come to what was apparently a false conclusion. "Beth said you were coming here to interview me. I assumed it was for an article." She glared at him. "And that's what you let me think." Then a sick thought struck her. Had Harmons College sent him? And he was still lying to her to cover up his real purpose. She wanted to order him out of her house. But she needed to find out what was really going on. Raising her chin, she demanded, "What murder? What are you doing investigating me?"

"There are some questions about Esther Knight's death. I'm interviewing everyone who knew her well. Naturally, you're on the list."

She felt a surge of relief. This had nothing to do with the damn college, but with poor Esther's death. Immediately she felt guilty.

To hide her own discomfort, she pinned Mr. Zachary Grant with some pointed questions. "That's how you work? By pretending to be someone you're not? And poking in my dresser drawers?"

"I was going to tell you I was a P.I."

"When? After you searched my bedroom?"

He had the grace to look even more embarrassed.

Her eyes flicked to the bed, and she was vastly relieved that at least the vibrator was hidden under the pillow.

Or had he found it and shoved it back?

She shifted her weight from one foot to the other, thinking she could be in a lot of trouble now. She'd let this guy into her house under obviously false pretenses. And she was alone with him. The only thing that made her feel the least little bit okay with the situation was that he'd won over Beth. Well, she was going to have a nice little chat with *her* as soon as she got rid of Mr. Snoop.

"Please leave," she said again.

To her relief, he said, "Okay."

She let out a breath, just as he brushed past her to get to the door.

His arm briefly touched her breast, and she made a startled sound in reaction.

She saw the set of his shoulders tighten as he marched down the hall. She was hoping he'd head out the front door. But he stopped in the living room.

"I'm sorry we got off on the wrong foot," he said.

"Oh, are you? Well, that's not my fault."

"I know." Reaching into his pocket, he pulled out a card and wrote something on the back. "I'm staying in town at the Duck Blind Motel. If there's anything you want to tell me, you can reach me there until tomorrow morning."

"Don't count on it."

"I'm not," he said stiffly as he hesitated at the door. He turned to look at her, his face a mixture of emotions.

"If Esther was murdered, then you could be in danger."

She bristled. "Are you trying to scare me? So you'll get me to keep talking to you?"

"I'm telling you to be careful. That's all."

She didn't even know what that meant.

"She lived in New York. I'm down here in a small town on the eastern shore of Maryland."

He nodded, then asked, "Have you seen a white van parked around here?"

"There are a lot of white vans on the road. Remember the police found that out in that sniper case in Washington, D.C."

His eyes met hers. "I saw one parked outside a while ago. When I walked over, whoever was inside drove away. So report anything suspicious to the police. I wouldn't want something to happen to you."

"You don't even know me."

"I form quick impressions of people."

"So do I," she snapped. "And I can tell you for certain that this interview is over."

"You have my number. If you get into any trouble, call me."

He was the last person on earth she was going to call, she thought as he walked through the door and closed it.

Somehow, while he was in the room, she'd kept herself together. The moment he was out of the house, she felt her knees weaken, and she had to lean against the door to stay on her feet.

Zachary Grant had taken her in so completely that he'd left her head spinning. And then he'd tried to scare her. Well, at least he was gone.

TONY HAD GONE home and changed vehicles. Now his stolen car was parked half a block away under the low-hanging branches of a tree where he watched the man leave little Miss O'Neal's house.

Probably she insisted that people call her Dr. O'Neal because she thought so much of herself. And why not, she was now writing one of the most popular columns in *Vanessa*. He'd found that out from reading some articles he'd discovered in an online search.

The editor couldn't let the column die, so when she'd lost Esther Knight, she'd gone looking for another know-it-all bitch. And she'd hit on Amanda O'Neal.

He'd watched her through the window, saw her going through that pile of letters unsuspecting women were sending her so she could meddle in their lives.

Of course, *Vanessa* wanted to keep her identity a secret—to protect the guilty. But he'd bugged the editor's phone. And when she'd driven to Maryland, he'd known she was going down there to hire the next Esther Scott.

His attention switched from the woman inside the house to her visitor.

He'd watched the guy get out of his burgundy Honda with the New Jersey license. Twice.

First he'd come strolling toward the van, and Tony had taken off. But he'd come back to find out what was going on—in time to see the guy disappearing into the house.

Tony had carefully taken down the license number of the Honda. He would have liked to have had a look inside the car, but it was too close to the house, so he couldn't take the chance that someone might glance out the window.

The car was aimed in the opposite direction from where Tony was sitting in his car now. He was betting that the guy wasn't going to make a U-turn when he left, because he was already facing toward the main road. And his assumption proved to be correct.

The guy roared away, and Tony breathed out a small sigh. Back to business as usual. Actually, not really. He'd been planning to wait a few days before he made his move. All at once he was thinking that it would be a good idea to speed up his timetable.

AMANDA STIFFENED her knees, then walked to the window, watching the duplicitous Mr. Grant get into his car and drive away. Then she couldn't stop herself from looking for a white van. Which she didn't see.

Pulling back from the front window, she turned and marched to the desk, where she picked up her phone book. Then she called New York.

"I'd like to speak to Beth Cantro," she told the receptionist.

"Whom shall I say is calling?"

"Amanda O'Neal. I'm returning her call," she added.

She waited, tapping her foot on the floor until her friend came on the line.

It was more than a minute before Beth answered, and Amanda imagined her finishing up a conference with one of her staffers.

"Amanda! How are you? Did you get the little present I sent you?" she asked.

"Are you talking about Zachary Grant?" she asked as she sat down in the desk chair.

"Yes, isn't he delicious?" Beth asked with a lilt

in her voice. "It was tempting to keep him for my-self."

"He's good-looking," she said carefully. "But... but from your phone message, I thought he'd come down here to do a magazine or a newspaper article. And he didn't bother to set me straight. Then I found him going through my dresser drawers."

"Oh, goodness. He seemed like a nice guy. And so yummy-looking."

"His looks are beside the point. He's not exactly ethical."

There was a long silence on the end of the line. "Maybe by his standards he is. I mean, don't detectives use all kinds of techniques? Haven't you seen those cop shows where they get the suspect to admit he's guilty by pretending they have evidence they don't really have?"

Amanda took the receiver away from her ear and stared at it for a second as if she could see through the instrument to her friend's face. Sometimes she wondered how Beth could have gotten to be the editor of a major magazine—when her logic could be so strange.

"What does any of that have to do with me?" she asked. "He doesn't think I'm guilty of anything, does he?"

"I didn't mean that he did. I was just giving an example."

"Okay."

"Don't dismiss him so quickly."

"Didn't you hear me? He was snooping through my stuff."

On the other end of the line, Beth took a moment

before answering. "You know I have pretty good instincts about people. He's a good guy."

"Oh, sure."

Amanda put forward another argument. Beth countered it. They went on for several minutes in that fashion, and Amanda finally decided there was going to be no way to convince Beth otherwise. In fact, by the end of the conversation, she had let Beth persuade her that Zachary Grant was only doing his job.

When she hung up, she was wondering how she'd let Beth talk her out of her legitimate indignation.

AFTER HIS ENCOUNTER with Dr. O'Neal, Zach wasn't feeling particularly hungry, but he didn't want to hang around his motel room, so he went down to the seafood restaurant on the St. Stephens dock. It was a large wooden building with several dining rooms, and he asked for a window seat where he could look out over the water. He'd always liked eating a meal in a waterfront restaurant. Maybe that went back to when he'd been a kid and his parents had taken the whole Grant brood for a day trip to the Jersey shore.

As he drank a bottle of Flying Duck beer, and picked at a crab cake sandwich, he looked out at the harbor, watching two swans fight a flotilla of ducks for bread crumbs being thrown to them by tourists.

He'd screwed up royally with the pretty blond sexual advice columnist. She'd thrown him badly off balance. As he'd read through the folder he'd accumulated on her, he'd decided that interviewing a woman who gave sexual advice was going to be intimidating. Then she'd opened her door, and he'd felt his chest go tight.

She'd looked too young and vulnerable to fill the

role he'd assigned her. And when they'd started talking, his impressions had done another flip-flop.

As first he hadn't acknowledged what he was feeling. But now that he was several miles and several hours away with a beer in his hand, he could admit how attracted he'd been to her. It had been a long time since he'd let himself get involved with a woman—and the sexual context of the interview had started working on him.

He grimaced. Being turned on by her was damn inconvenient. And now he had a long evening ahead of him. Maybe he should remind himself that she'd known Esther Knight since graduate school. Maybe he should remind himself that she had a lot to gain by taking over the column. But he simply couldn't see her having any ulterior motives.

Sitting at the restaurant table, he thought about how he admired the way she'd recovered from her shock at seeing him rummaging in her bedroom drawer. She had guts. But what if he'd really been a pervert? Then she should have gotten the hell out of the house. But she'd stood her ground.

He should warn her about the value of cutting and running when you were in a tight situation. Only he wasn't going to get a chance. He'd be going back to New Jersey tomorrow. Back to work, because he'd finished what he needed to do down here.

The problem was, he didn't love the work. He'd liked being a cop a lot better. But he'd changed his profession to please his wife. He'd opened his own one-man agency, and taken whatever assignments walked in the door because he and Mindy had needed the money. Then the marriage had blown up in his face, and he'd just drifted along doing the same old thing.

But he'd been thinking recently that he was ready to go back to the police force. He wanted assignments that were more worthwhile and challenging than getting the goods on cheating husbands and wives or people working insurance scams. Like this murder investigation, for example. Not that many murder cases came his way. This was the most exciting job he'd had in a couple of months.

Or maybe it was Amanda that was exciting him. He wished to hell he could tell the difference.

After paying for his meal, he killed some time by driving around St. Stephens. As he headed west, he considered going back to O'Neal's house and checking to see if that white van was there again. Then he pictured her catching him driving past.

With a shake of his head, he went back to his hotel and paid for a movie that he hoped would distract him.

He picked a guy flick, with plenty of action. Then the hero climbed in to bed with a beautiful spy and Zach found himself getting hot as he put himself and Dr. O'Neal into the bedroom scene.

He moved his shoulder uncomfortably on the bed, thinking there was no reason he couldn't do something about the hard-on straining behind the fly of his slacks.

Hadn't Amanda O'Neal given him permission to enjoy his sexuality—any way that worked for him?

But he couldn't get her image out of his mind. It was almost like she was standing there beside the bed, watching him. And he wasn't going to jerk off in front of her.

When his gaze flicked back to the television, he found that a truckful of explosives was about to crash into a nuclear power plant. Good, that should prove sufficient distraction to take his mind off the lower part of his body.

AMANDA HAD MADE herself a tuna salad for dinner, but she'd finally put most of the salad into the refrigerator. If she'd been at Harmons College, she would have called one of her girlfriends and gone out to dinner and maybe a movie. Her friend Jane Baxter in the sociology department or Carolyn Martin who was also in psychology. They would have discussed the whole thing. Zach. The murder case. Her reactions. His reactions. Maybe she'd even have been able to laugh over the vibrator.

She'd had a pretty good support system at the college. Until the scandal had made a lot of people start avoiding her. Not Jane and Carolyn, though. She'd been the one to avoid them because she'd been too down on herself. And she hadn't wanted the scandal to rub off on them. Now she wished she hadn't broken the ties. But she couldn't just call them out of the blue because she had a guy to discuss. So she was on her own.

To fill the time, she went back to the column. Beth had asked her how it was coming, and she'd said she was almost ready to turn it in. Now she had to make that claim a reality.

But she found it as difficult to concentrate now as she had that afternoon. Only now it was worse. After assuring herself that her vibrator was still under her pillow, she'd put it back in her drawer.

Holding it had made her previous arousal return.

Only now there was nothing she could do about it. Because when she lay down on the bed, she couldn't banish the picture in her mind of Zachary Grant. He was too handsome. Too vital. Too complicated. Too interesting to her.

Unfortunately, she didn't have as much actual dating experience as most women her age. First she'd been focused on getting her Ph.D. Then she'd found that men were intimidated by a woman who'd made human sexuality her specialty.

Well—either intimidated or eager to take advantage of her supposed experience.

She'd sensed that Zachary was nervous. And she'd tried to put him at ease. But perhaps she'd gone about it the wrong way—by babbling on about her theories of human sexuality.

Was that why he'd gotten caught going through her dresser drawers? Because he'd *wanted* to be caught. So she'd throw him out—and that would end the relationship.

That was kind of convoluted thinking. Yet as a psychologist, she knew that people often did things that they couldn't explain on a conscious level.

Take herself, for example, she thought with a twist of her mouth. She was lying here going into Byzantine psychological explanations for Zachary's behavior—when she knew what she was really doing was trying to convince her body that thinking about him wasn't making her hot and tingly.

She might be composing a psych paper in her head, but her nipples were hard, and the hot, swollen feeling between her legs was certainly annoying.

She moved restlessly on the bed, glanced toward the drawer with the vibrator, then looked quickly away.

What she needed was some nice, calming deep breathing exercises.

Eyes closed, she made herself comfortable on the mattress, then took in a breath and held it for several seconds before slowly letting the air trickle from her lungs.

It had the quieting effect on her senses that she'd hoped for. And she did it again, focusing on the in and out passage of air from her body.

But just as she was about to suck in another breath, a noise outside made her go rigid.

It sounded like someone had knocked over a flowerpot on the patio. As she listened intently, her gaze shot to the clock on the bedside table. It was almost midnight.

Should she call the police? And say what—that a detective had come here to interview her and made her nervous?

She could just imagine how that would go over. It wasn't difficult to picture the cops having a good time laughing in her face.

One officer in particular. The one who had pulled her over for speeding when she'd first arrived in St. Stephens.

Apparently the locals knew that the traffic patrol lay in wait for speeders along Route 50. But nobody had bothered to tell her—until she'd heard a siren and seen the flashing red-and-blue lights in her rearview mirror.

The trooper who had pulled her over had been excruciatingly polite—which hadn't done anything to convince her that he wasn't having a perfectly wonderful time looking at her breasts as he explained her infraction.

No, she wasn't going to call the police and chance having that same guy show up at her door.

So she closed her eyes and focused on her breathing again. She was just starting to relax when another sound made her body jerk off the mattress.

This time it wasn't a flowerpot. This time she heard the knob on the French doors to the patio slowly twisting.

4

AMANDA'S HEART leaped into her throat as she sat up in bed and reached for the phone, along with the business card Zachary Grant had given her.

She'd intended to throw it in the trash. But some impulse had made her set it on the bedside table. She had never believed in fate. Until now.

There was enough light coming in the window from the streetlight outside for her to see the number he'd written on the back.

When she got the motel, she asked for room 255.

"Zachary, thank God," she blurted when he picked up the phone.

"Amanda, what's wrong?"

"There's someone outside on my patio."

"Where are you?"

"In the bedroom."

"Lock the door. And call the police. I'll be right there," he clipped out the words, then hung up.

She was left clutching the phone in the darkness.

Lord, how far away was the Duck Blind Motel? How long would it take him to get here?

There was another noise from the front of the house, this time the sound of the patio door opening.

With her pulse pounding in her throat, she jumped out of bed ran to the bedroom door and locked it. But how much good would that do her?

She was about to call the police when she heard footsteps coming down the hall. Heavy footsteps. A man's footsteps.

Then someone tried to turn the knob on the bedroom door and, after discovering it was locked, started kicking the door.

She was dressed only in the long T-shirt she'd worn to bed. But she didn't hesitate to leap to the window and flip the lock open.

After pushing up the double sash, she pushed the screen out with her bare foot and climbed through.

Luckily the bedroom of the small house was on the ground floor. It was only three feet down to the flower bed, where she stood for a moment feeling dazed.

The sound of the bedroom door bursting open galvanized her to action. Dashing down the drive, she fled into the underbrush at the side of the road, stones digging painfully into her bare feet.

When headlights cut through the darkness, she stepped to the shoulder, waving. The car slowed and Zachary rolled down his window.

"He's in the house," she shouted to him.

"Did you call the cops?"

"Not yet."

"Do it."

Zachary pulled to the curb, sprinted up the drive, then disappeared around the side of the house.

Her cell phone was back inside, in the charging cradle. And she wasn't about to go back to get it. The neighborhood was fairly rural, and the closest house was fifty yards away. Wishing she had on more clothing, she ran down the road to her nearest neighbor and banged on the front door. Ten seconds later, an upstairs window opened.

"What's all that racket?" a man's voice called into the night. "I've got a gun."

She was glad the porch roof was between her and the weapon. Or would that make any difference?

"There's an intruder at my house," she yelled out. "Just down the road. Call 9-1-1."

The window banged shut, and she didn't know whether the guy was going to do the right thing or not. So much for small-town neighborliness.

Turning back toward her house, she wondered what to do now. Zachary had disappeared inside, and she realized suddenly that he had put himself in danger—for her.

With her bottom lip between her teeth, she stood, staring at the front door as though that would give her insight into what was going on inside.

She could go in there. But it was likely that she wasn't going to be much help. Maybe she'd even make things worse.

Still, she took a step closer and then another.

She jumped back and screamed when the front door flew open and a man emerged and fled across the lawn.

Seconds later, Zachary appeared—and took off after him. The two men disappeared in the darkness beside the river.

When she heard Zachary curse, she ran toward the sound of his voice and found him picking himself up from the ground, just as a car engine started somewhere nearby.

"What happened?" she asked.

"I tripped over a damn tree root, and the bastard got away."

"Are you all right?"

"Fine," he snapped, striding back toward her house.

She followed, limping slightly now because the bottoms of her feet hurt. When she'd stepped into the living room, Zachary closed the door, then turned to face her.

Hours ago, she'd told him to get out. Another man in the same position wouldn't have felt compelled to rush over and rescue her. "Why did you go after him?" she asked softly, taking a step toward him.

He didn't answer, only moved toward her, and they met in the middle of the living room.

Reaching out, she clasped her arms around him. She wasn't even sure why. To comfort herself? To tell him how grateful she was? To let him know how relieved she was that nothing serious had happened to him?

Now that the danger was over, she had started to shake.

"You're fine. Everything's okay," he murmured, his hands soothing over her back and shoulders.

When she lifted her face to his, staring up into his dark eyes, the emotions of the moment overwhelmed her. "I got...got out of the house all right," she stammered. "Then you went in. And I was scared for you."

He looked down at her for a long moment. Then his eyes focused on her lips. She could have pulled back. But when he lowered his head toward hers, she raised up on tiptoes—meeting again halfway.

She'd always considered kissing a pleasant activity. She would never have labeled this kiss as merely pleasant.

The first mouth-to-mouth contact was like a bolt of

electricity, sizzling along her nerve endings, swamping her mind and body.

She discovered very quickly that Zachary Grant knew how to kiss—with his lips, his tongue, his teeth. He was sensual and masterful, subtle and overwhelming by turns. And thoroughly absorbed in what he was doing, as though kissing were an end in itself.

She'd met few men like that. Usually kissing was a prelude to sex. Or that's what they wanted it to be.

But she sensed that for Zachary Grant, it was an activity to be enjoyed for its own sake.

She made a small needy sound as she drank in the heady taste of the man who held her so firmly in his arms. She clung to him while he angled his head, first one way and then the other, as though he were greedy to experience her every way he could—and greedy to take the kiss to levels she'd never thought possible in mouth-to-mouth contact.

But it wasn't enough. Not for her. And apparently not for him, either. She felt one of his large hands slide down to her hips and slip under the hem of her T-shirt to pull her lower body in against his erection, as though he were desperate to satisfy his craving for intimate contact with her.

The other hand flattened against her back, pressing her breasts against his chest.

She had never lost her head with a man—always been cautious in her relationships. She had never been as hot and needy as she was now. Really, she had been hot and needy since he'd interrupted her in the bedroom the afternoon before.

Now—

Now she suddenly remembered why he'd knocked on her door and why she had thrown him out of the house the last time he'd been here. She also remembered she was wearing little more than a long T-shirt.

Breaking the kiss, she pressed her hands against his shoulders, then watched his gaze come back into focus.

Still, he didn't turn her loose.

"You're getting out of here," he said, as though there were no room for argument.

Her brain struggled to make sense of the command. "I can't."

"What do you mean, you can't?"

"I rented this house for six months."

"Staying here isn't a great idea," he said in a voice that left no room for argument. "I was hired to find out what happened to Esther Knight. She's dead. Now you're in danger. Have you made any enemies in town?"

"I haven't been here long enough to make enemies."

"Then we're back to a link with Esther Knight."

"Or someone who targeted a woman living alone."

"Either way, a bad guy was staking out your place. I told you I saw a white van hanging around this afternoon. I saw it drive away again tonight."

"The same van?"

He hesitated. "I can't be one hundred percent sure. As you reminded me, there are a lot of white vans on the road." He looked toward the window. "By the way, where are the cops? Didn't you call them?"

"I asked a neighbor to do it. He threatened to shoot me."

"Friendly guy."

"We could call the police now," she said.

"We can do that later. Right now, I'm moving you out of here."

She tipped her head to one side, trying to wrap her head around his words and the brittle tone of his voice. "Why? Why should you get involved?"

She saw him swallow. He turned away and walked toward the window, looking out into the darkness. His shoulders were hunched, and she could tell from his body language that whatever he had to say wasn't coming easily. "I don't want to make the same mistake I did last time," he finally said.

The answer was so unexpected that she blinked. "Last time what?"

"Last time I let a woman get harmed because I was too blind to understand what was happening."

"I think you'd better explain that."

He nodded, then pivoted to face her. "I used to be a police detective. But when I got married, my wife, Mindy, thought the job was too dangerous. So I started a P.I. business."

Her fingers went to her lips as the memory of the kiss sizzled through her. "You're married?" she said in a voice that she couldn't hold steady.

"Not anymore. A thug I'd put in prison got out and decided to even the score. He kidnapped Mindy. I figured out where he was holding her. The cops and I got her back. But she was...pretty traumatized. After that, the marriage was over. We've been divorced for more than a year."

"Oh."

"So I'm getting you out of this house. Tonight."

"Because you feel guilty?" she asked carefully.

"Because I care about you."

She could remind him that they barely knew each

other. But she didn't do it—for several reasons that she didn't want to examine too closely. But first and foremost, she knew she'd be a fool to send him on his way when he was offering to protect her.

"We could both stay here," she said.

"We could. But I've been up for over twenty-four hours. I need some sleep. And I'll feel better about getting it if I know the guy who broke in doesn't know your location."

"All right."

"Pack some clothes."

"Everything?"

"Just enough for a few days."

"And my work."

"Yes."

"Where are we going?"

"To the Duck Blind Motel."

"To your room?"

He looked at his watch. "The office is closed. My room will have to do for tonight. Then we'll think of something else."

She didn't want to be locked in a motel room with Zachary Grant. The idea seemed much too intimate. But what he was saying made sense.

He followed her down the hall. When she got to her bedroom, she stopped short. A chair lay on its side. And the bedcovers were hanging off on the floor.

"What happened in here?" she asked.

"He and I got into it. Unfortunately, he shoved me onto the bed and beat it," he said in a clipped tone, and she realized he didn't want to discuss the details.

Repressing further questions, she pulled on a pair of sweatpants and athletic shoes, then hurriedly packed some clothing. When she returned to the living room, she stuffed the letters back into their mail sack. All she had to do then was put her laptop back into its case.

"Ready?" Zach asked.

"As ready as I will be," she answered. Following him out of the house, she locked the door, then wondered what good that would do.

A feeling of unreality gripped her as she climbed into his car.

"I guess the motel is pretty close," she said.

"Yes, but we're not going straight there. I've got to make sure nobody is following us."

She answered with a tight nod, thinking that she'd put herself into this man's hands. Now she was having second thoughts about her hasty decision.

She tried to relax as he headed for the highway, then took another exit back into town—his attention divided between the road ahead and the rearview mirror.

It was after one in the morning now, and there was little traffic on the road. As far as she could tell, there were no white vans—or anybody else—following them.

Finally, he pulled into the parking lot of a small, nondescript motel on Route 50.

His room was at one end. After he'd turned on the light and helped her carry her stuff inside, she looked around at the small space. There was a queen-size bed, a table and two inexpensive armchairs by the window, a dresser with the requisite television set and not much else.

The first words she heard herself saying were, "We can't both sleep in that bed."

"I can sleep in a chair," he shot back, crossing the room and pulling one of the chairs around so that it faced the other.

His back was to her, and she watched the tight set of his shoulders, wondering what to say. She'd always been better at writing than talking. And lately she wasn't doing so well at that, either.

Still with his back to her, he cleared his throat. "Dear Esther," he said, and she wondered if she'd heard him right.

"Dear Esther," he said again. "I find myself in rather a strange situation. I'm in a motel room with a woman I'm very attracted to. But we don't know each other real well. And I know she's nervous about what I might do. That's my fault—because I kissed her, which I know I shouldn't have done. But I was worried about her when someone broke in to her house, and when I saw that she was okay, I hugged her. And that turned into a kiss. But now I'd like to convince her that I'm not going to step out of line." He paused for several heartbeats, then said, "Signed, Worried in St. Stephens."

She stood there, watching his tense stance. He had just revealed a lot to her. Things he'd most likely found hard to say. And now she had to answer him.

She licked her dry lips, then began, "Dear Worried in St. Stephens, uh…telling her what you're thinking makes all the difference. I know it's difficult to say personal things to a woman you don't know well. But you did it. And that takes away the worry about being alone with you."

She heard him heave a deep sigh, but he didn't turn back to face her. So she walked to the bed, straightened the covers and took off her shoes. Keeping her sweatpants and T-shirt on, she lay down.

When he started toward the chairs, she said, "You need to sleep. You're not going to be very comfortable over there."

He turned to face her, his gaze questioning.

"This bed is pretty wide. I think we can manage."

"You're sure?"

"Yes."

She watched him turn off the light, then kick off his shoes. The mattress shifted. When her eyes had grown accustomed to the darkness, she slid him a look. He was lying on the far edge of the bed, still wearing the clothing he'd pulled on before rushing to her house.

He looked stiff and uncomfortable. But she wasn't going to invite him to get undressed. Instead, she focused on trying to get some sleep—which she was sure she would never be able to do because she was too aware of the man lying next to her.

Dear Esther, she thought. *Is it possible for a man and a woman who are attracted to each other to share the same bed and not end up making love? Signed, Curious in St. Stephens.*

Dear Curious, she answered her own question. *Of course it's possible for a man and a woman who are attracted to each other to be in close proximity and agree not to engage in hanky-panky.*

Hanky-panky. That was a nice old-fashioned term. Still it got her thinking that all she'd have to do was move her arm a little and her hand would brush Zachary's. That brought a wave of heat sweeping over her body, and she knew she was in trouble.

She'd told him to get into bed with her. Now she

had to keep her cool. On the other side of the mattress, he shifted uncomfortably, and she wondered if he was having the same problem. When she found herself staring at the front of his chinos to try and see if he had an erection, she clamped her teeth together. What had she been *thinking* when she'd invited him to bed?

She'd sentenced herself to lying here for the rest of the night, hot and needy and obsessing about whether she was the only one suffering. But some time during the next hour, she drifted off to sleep. And some time later, a low, choking sound woke her again.

5

ALARMED BY THE SOUND of distress, Amanda pressed her back against the mattress, trying to figure out where she was and why.

It was dark, with only a narrow shaft of light coming in between the curtains, and it took a moment for her fogged brain to remember that she was in a motel room bed—and why there was a man lying next to her.

His body jerked, and she shifted toward him. "Zachary?"

He didn't answer. He appeared to be asleep. But his head moved from side to side on the pillow, and she knew that he was in the grip of a nightmare.

"It's all right. Zachary, wake up."

When he didn't answer, she slid over and laid a hand on his warm, muscular shoulder.

She knew immediately that she'd made a big mistake. He was still in the grip of a nightmare, but he reacted instantly. Flipping her to her back, he came down heavily on top of her, his big body pressing hers into the mattress.

Instinctively, she flailed against the weight of his chest pressed to hers. At the same time, she tried to let him know where he was and whom he was with.

"Zachary! It's Amanda. We're in your hotel room. Please…Zachary, you're scaring me," she gasped.

One minute he was on top of her. In the next, his weight lifted. But she sensed him hovering over her, looking down at her in the darkness.

"Amanda. Amanda, I'm so sorry. Are you all right?"

"Yes. But you...frightened me."

"Oh, Christ! I'm so sorry," he repeated, his voice raw, and she knew he hated what he'd just done.

"What happened?" she asked, making an effort to speak normally.

He heaved a sigh. "The guy. The kidnapper. I was trying to stop him from getting away. Then you woke me up—only he wasn't here. And you were."

He turned on the light beside the bed. Although the bulb was low, they both blinked in the sudden illumination.

"You mean the man who kidnapped your wife?" she asked.

"Yeah. I guess what happened tonight brought it all back. I was dreaming about him, but it was all mixed up. In the dream he'd kidnapped you, and I was frantic to find you."

"Oh," she breathed, thinking about how she'd figured into the bad dream.

"Then I did. He and I were fighting. Only you were in the wrong place at the wrong time. My bed, to be exact. And I was going after you—not him."

The look of remorse clouding his features and the anguish in his voice tore at her. Her fingers stroked up and down his arm, but he pulled away from her and flopped to his back, pressing his hand to his forehead.

"I'm dangerous," he muttered.

"No."

"What do you mean—no? I attacked you."

"Well, you started to. But you didn't do any damage. You stopped as soon as you knew it was me."

"Thank God!" He turned his head toward her. "Why aren't you climbing out of this bed and running screaming in the other direction?"

"Because I know you're a good man, Zachary Grant—whether you want to admit it or not."

"Oh yeah, how do you know?"

"Because I'm a trained psychologist. I'm a good judge of character."

He made a dismissive sound. "Why did I sense that you didn't much like finding me snooping in your room?"

She hoped the light wasn't bright enough to reveal the stain that spread across her cheeks. "You were doing your job—as you saw it. You wanted information about me, and you took an opportunity that presented itself."

"You've sure changed your tune."

It sounded like he was determined to make her say something negative about him. If so, he was going to be disappointed. Into the darkened bedroom, she said, "If you were an insensitive jerk, you wouldn't be having nightmares about your wife's kidnapping. You would have gotten over it."

He snorted. "Former wife."

She realized that words weren't going to make him feel better. He had an answer for every argument she put forth. Stretching out her arm, she found his hand and clasped it. That was the only place they touched, just a few inches of his warm skin against hers, yet she felt as though she'd bridged a continental gulf.

Neither of them spoke. There were so many things

she wanted to say, but she didn't think he'd believe her. He'd been through a terrible experience. People were shaped by the things that happened to them. His wife had reacted one way. He'd reacted another.

He'd been hurt and felt scared and guilty. With her training, she was sure she could help him. If he would let her. Which she knew wasn't a sure thing.

But that wasn't her only motivation. There was something for her here, too. She sensed that *he* could help *her*. They hadn't known each other long. Still, there was something about her relationship with him that was different from any man she'd met before in her life. Was it because he was the most frankly sexual man she'd ever been with?

She sighed. Or because she found him so appealing? She remembered lecturing him about relationships. Well, they seemed to have one. And she wanted to explore that. She wanted to find out what they meant to each other and what they might mean. For now she lay with him in bed, their fingers barely touching. It was such a minimal contact, yet she sensed its importance—to both of them.

IN THE DARKNESS of the motel bedroom, Amanda's role had seemed clear. In the morning she wasn't quite so certain of where she stood with Zachary—or where she wanted to stand.

She was pretending to be asleep when she felt the mattress shift. Through slitted eyes, she saw him stand beside the bed, then walk rapidly to the bathroom. Through the closed door, she heard him getting dressed. Then he vacated the bathroom and exited the room—she assumed to give her some privacy while she got up.

She wanted to tell him that they should just act normally. But she was too unsettled to know what normal was. So she focused on the simple task of getting dressed.

She had just emerged from the bathroom when he came back into the room and closed the door, so she knew he must have been waiting right outside.

"Hi," she said.

He shifted his weight from one foot to the other. "Are you all right?"

"Yes."

"Good. I'm going to pick us up some breakfast. And take care of some other things. So don't worry if I don't come right back. Put the chain on the door, and don't let anyone but me in."

"Okay."

"What do you want to eat?"

"Something easy. A fast-food breakfast sandwich."

"I can handle that."

After setting the chain and making the bed, she got out her computer and some letters. But she hardly got any work done in the hour he was gone.

She kept looking toward the door. And she leaped up when he knocked. When she opened the door, he came in, carrying bags with a familiar logo.

Quickly she cleared the table of her work, and they both sat down.

After he'd unpacked egg and bacon sandwich muffins, orange juice and strong coffee, they both ate in silence for several minutes.

"Is this your usual breakfast?" she asked.

"I never got over liking eggs and bacon, even when the health gurus said they were bad for you."

"Me, too."

They grinned at each other, sharing their secret passion for cholesterol before going back to the food.

When she looked up again, she saw him turning a foam cup between his hands.

"What?"

"We should talk business," he said.

"Oh?" she said, hearing the catch in her own voice.

"I stopped by the police station and reported the incident last night. So they're aware of the situation. They're willing to swing by your house periodically."

"You...uh...sound like you have that under control."

"Yeah, well, it helps establish my credibility with them that I'm a former cop." He laughed. "And that I wasn't kicked off the force."

She nodded.

"But they're a small department, and they can't devote a lot of resources to a break-in at a rental property."

"Does that make a difference? I mean, that I'm renter."

"It shouldn't. But when they've got their own townspeople and tourists to take care of—their own people are going to come first."

"The tourists are just for catching in speed traps," she muttered, remembering her experience with one of the boys in blue.

Ignoring her comment, he went on. "Anyway, I wouldn't recommend staying where you are. My best suggestion would be for you to make the company that rented you the house aware of the situation—then get them to let you select another property."

She shifted in her seat. "You think they'd agree?"

"Yeah. If you give up your river view."

When he saw her hesitate, he went on, "I can work the switch for you. Actually, it would be better if I go into the real estate office and talk to them."

"Why are you doing all this?"

"I'd like to feel you're safe when I leave."

So he was leaving. Well, there was no reason for him to stay. Fighting back a wave of disappointment, she gave a tight nod. She'd been having fantasies about this man, and it was time to lay them to rest. In a strong voice, she said, "Okay, if you can get me another house, I'd be grateful."

"Which real estate company did you work through?"

"Monarch."

"Okay." He took another swallow of coffee, then set down the cup on the table and stood. "You stay here out of sight. Same rules. Put the chain back on the door when I leave. Keep the blinds closed, and don't let anyone in. I'll be back as soon as I can."

After he'd left her alone again, she took a shower, washed and dried her hair and changed into a clean T-shirt and shorts.

Then she went back to the mail.

It was difficult to work, but she had to finish her column, and reading letters would distract her from her own problems.

The first one she opened said—

Dear Esther,
My boyfriend is talking about getting married. But I'm not sure that's such a great idea. He's a lot more adventuresome sexually than I am.

Like, he wants to tie me up. And sometimes he calls me up and starts talking real sexy on the phone. And I don't know how to handle that either.

Can you tell me what to do?

Confused in Wisconsin

Amanda read over the letter, then laid it back on top of the stack. Another bondage question. This one for her—not the former Esther Scott.

She sighed. Was it a lot more prevalent than she'd assumed? Truly, she wasn't sure what to answer, since she'd never tried either bondage or phone sex.

She didn't want to think about bondage. What about phone sex? Was it healthy? The woman hadn't said that her boyfriend went away on trips. Was he calling from across the city? The next state? What?

Maybe she should go on to another letter. Then a knock at the door made her jump.

She got up and pulled the curtains aside. Zachary was standing on the narrow cement strip outside.

Quickly she reached for the chain and slid it out of the metal bracket, then opened the door.

Zachary was grinning as he stepped into the room. "Good news," he said.

"I've got you a nice new house. It's on Turtle Creek, so that's not the river. But you've got an extra bedroom. And a bigger kitchen."

"How did you manage that?"

"Charm."

She laughed. "Yeah. Right. You saw the place?"

"Briefly. But I'm not the one who has to sign on the dotted line. You can back out if you don't like it."

"Okay."

"Let's get you packed up again. If you like the house, we can collect the rest of your belongings later. You've got a few days overlap—to give you time to move."

She marveled at his take-charge attitude. Apparently when Zachary Grant decided to get something done—he did it.

He strode toward the table, then stopped when he saw the letter. She'd told him the correspondence was confidential. When he glanced at her, she gave a tiny shrug. Permission, if that's how he wanted to take it.

She wasn't sure why she was giving that permission. Because she wanted his opinion on the subject?

She watched him bend to read the text.

"So, are you going to tell her it's okay to try bondage?" he asked in a conversational tone.

"That could be dangerous."

"It sounds like they're in a committed relationship."

"I can't tell for sure. Sometimes, when readers give the background of a relationship, they're misleading."

"Why?"

"A lot of different reasons. They could be describing something they wished they had. Or they could be embarrassed to tell me that they're doing very intimate things with a guy they barely know."

He tipped his head to one side, considering that. "They'd lie to you? In a letter to a magazine columnist?"

"They might."

He tapped the letter. "But in any case, you don't approve of bondage?"

"I think that a woman should be cautious about letting a guy tie her up."

"Well, there's always the phone sex angle."

She resisted the impulse to fold her arms across her chest. "Why is phone sex better than the real thing?"

"Why not? Sometimes people can communicate better on the phone than they can in person."

"Why do you think that is?" she pressed.

He took a moment before answering. "I find it's true in my work. Sometimes people can tell me things that they might not be able to say face-to-face. The phone makes the encounter safer because the other person can't see your reactions. That's why I think that those science fiction movies where people talk on picture phones are a bunch of crap. Picture phones will never catch on because people like the anonymity." He laughed. "And what woman is going to talk on a picture phone if she hasn't fixed her hair and put on her makeup?"

She laughed with him. "You have a point." Then she steered the conversation back to the subject. "But if you interview someone and it's not face-to-face, aren't you missing important clues?"

He tipped his head to one side, as he regarded her. "Yeah, you're right, I do miss something. It's easier to lie when the other person can't see your face. But I can key in on other stuff—tone of voice, even a little catch in a person's speech can be revealing."

There were some aspects of his job that were like hers, she thought.

Before she could comment on that, he turned away from her, pushed the letters into a pile, and put them back into the bag. While he got her work in order, she collected her toilet articles from the bathroom.

In less than five minutes, she was ready to leave.

He made her wait inside while he looked around the parking lot. When he motioned for her to get into his car, she remembered that her own vehicle was back at the old house.

"My car. I forgot my car is still back home."

"We'll get it later if you like the new place."

"Okay."

They drove out of town, with Zachary watching the rearview mirror as much as the road ahead. The house Amanda had rented was in a semirural neighborhood. This part of town was even more isolated, with large lots that fronted on a narrow country road. Some of the houses were in what she'd call the mansion category—what she could see of them through the trees.

She wasn't sure what to expect when Zachary turned in at a rural mailbox and drove up a rutted gravel lane. The road ended in a parking area in front of a storybook cottage.

"It's beautiful," she exclaimed.

"There are lots of great features," Zachary answered, as though he were a real estate agent. "There's a deck overlooking the creek. Like I said, there are two bedrooms instead of one. And the kitchen is something I imagine you'll enjoy."

"Is the rent the same?" she asked as they got out of the car.

"Yeah."

"You must be quite a salesman."

"Well I have to be. When people come in to hire a private detective, they're not always certain that's what they really want to do."

"Why not?"

"Deep down, they may not want to find out their

spouse is cheating on them. Or they may be concerned that I'll invade their privacy. You know, like poke around in their underwear drawers.''

''Oh.''

''But back to the real estate agency. The owner was very sorry about the break-in and very eager for you to be happy. Especially after I pointed out how flimsy the lock was on the sliding glass door.''

She watched him shift his weight from one foot to the other. ''What?''

''How would you feel if I hung around for a few days? Just to make sure everything's okay. I could use the spare bedroom.''

She felt her heart leap inside her chest. She'd thought he was leaving. Now he was offering to stay.

''I'd appreciate that,'' she murmured, trying not to let him see how glad she was that he'd changed his mind. ''But don't you have to get back to your work?''

''At the moment, my main job is for Esther Knight's family. I talked to them on the phone this morning and told them I might have an important lead. They can afford to pay me pretty well, so there's no problem about money.''

She was very conscious of the way he'd introduced the subject of his current assignment. He hadn't said he was on the trail of Esther Knight's killer, probably to keep the present author of the column from freaking out.

Instead of commenting on his choice of words, she said, ''Let's have a look at the inside of the house.''

''Sure. I've got two keys. One for you and one for me.''

So he'd thought she'd agree to his staying around,

she mused as they walked up three steps to a wide porch with two wicker rocking chairs grouped on either side of a low, round table.

Zachary unlocked the door, and they took a quick tour of the house. He'd chosen well. The rooms were bright and airy and furnished with comfortable but functional pieces. The master bedroom looked out over the deck and the creek. And the eat-in kitchen must have been remodeled within the past year.

"What do you think?" he asked.

"It's a great place."

"Are you sure they're giving it to me for the same rent?"

"Absolutely." He changed the subject quickly. "I'll go back to my room, pack my stuff and check out. Then I'll tell the real estate office you're taking this house."

"Shouldn't I do that?"

"I want you out of sight as much as possible. I'll bring the papers here for you to sign."

He walked to the phone, picked up the receiver and listened. "You've got a connection. That's good."

She saw a strange expression flit across his face.

"What?"

"I don't want you out of touch."

"Right."

He was being very matter of fact, yet she couldn't shake the feeling that he was pleased that she'd agreed to let him move in with her.

Was he *just* doing his job? Or was there more to it? Did he want to get to know her better? She was pretty sure that was true.

That thought had her conjuring up cozy pictures of

the two of them snuggled on the couch in front of the fireplace. Or outside in the hot tub on the deck.

Still, by the time he'd been gone for ten minutes, she was already having second thoughts. Was she making a big mistake? She hardly knew this man. But she'd let him rush her out of her rental house and into one of his own choosing. With him.

Because she was frightened of being killed? That was part of it, certainly. But she knew that the attraction between herself and Zachary Grant was just as important a factor. It was as if the break-in last night had given the two of them permission to do something neither one of them would have done under other circumstances. And they were both taking advantage of the opportunity fate had handed them.

She was restless, so she rummaged around the kitchen, seeing what equipment the owners of the property had provided.

Next she made a more thorough tour of the house, trying to decide where she wanted to set up her office area. There was a desk in the bedroom. That would give her privacy. But was privacy what she wanted? Or would it be interesting to discuss the letters with Zachary and get his input into the answers.

She wasn't sure she liked the direction her thoughts were taking. She'd signed a contract to write the column. She hadn't told Beth she was going to be using an assistant. And a man, at that.

Still, it would be valuable to have a guy's perspective. Like with that phone sex thing. He thought it was perfectly fine. She wasn't so sure.

When she realized her mind was zinging back to Zachary again, she grimaced, then hauled everything into the bedroom and set the laptop down on the desk.

The letter she'd been considering was still at the top of the stack. But she wasn't sure whether she wanted to answer it. So she opened more envelopes, pausing to glance up and look out the window.

She'd given up her river view. But Turtle Creek was beautiful, with trees and ferns dotting the bank. The geese liked it, too. A trio of the waterfowl landed on the water and began swimming around, looking for food.

She could watch the geese all day, she thought, but that wouldn't get her column written. Snatching up one of the letters she'd opened, she began to read:

Dear Esther,
I've had several sexual relationships in the past. They were good, but I always felt like something was missing. Now I've met a man who really turns me on. We have mind-blowing sex. I come so many times with him that I'm worn out after a weekend together.

But there are other things that concern me. Our backgrounds are really different. I'm in the corporate world. He drives a truck. I know my family would think that he's beneath me. And I don't know if our values are too different for us to make a life together. So what should I do? Is great sex enough for a relationship?

Dithering in Chicago

Amanda shifted in her seat, thinking about what it would be like coming so many times that you were worn out.

Usually with a guy or with her vibrator, she had one orgasm. She knew some women were able to have more, but she'd always been satisfied with what she had.

Now...

She clamped her teeth together. She was sitting here getting hot again. And when she thought about the letter writer and her boyfriend, the picture she got in her mind was of herself and Zachary Grant. What the heck was she going to do when Zachary came back? Jump his bones?

He wouldn't mind. But then what? How did they deal with each other. This house was larger than the last one, but it wasn't so big that two people wouldn't be constantly aware of each other.

Like now, she thought, as she heard the front door open and realized that most of what she'd been doing for the past hour was waiting for him to come back.

"Zachary? Is that you?" she called out.

He didn't answer, and she twisted around in her seat, looking down the hall. From her bedroom in the back, she couldn't see the front of the house, and a little frisson of fear went through her. Suppose it wasn't Zachary. Suppose it was the guy from last night?

When the phone rang, she jumped. It was on the bedside table, and she crossed the room to pick it up.

"Hello."

"Hi."

"Zachary? Where are you? There's somebody in the house," she said, hearing the quaver in her voice.

"It's me."

"But—what are you doing?"

"Sitting on the living room sofa," he answered, the simple sentence sounding provocative.

She stared down the hall, still unable to see him.

"If you're in the living room, why are you calling me?"

"Like I said, sometimes people can communicate better on the phone than they can in person."

She felt the air whoosh out of her lungs.

"Are we having trouble communicating?" she asked.

"Well, there are things I want to say to you. But I find my tongue getting all twisted up," he said.

She'd had similar feelings. "You do?" she whispered.

"Yeah."

He didn't continue, and she desperately wanted to find out what he meant. "What can't you say in person?"

"I'd like to kiss you again. I thought about that a lot while I was away. But if I did, maybe you wouldn't let me share this house with you. And I want to stay here with you—very much."

Her throat was so constricted that she could barely speak but she managed one syllable. "Why?"

"Because I'm worried about you. But we both know that's only part of it. I want to get to know you better. Only things haven't worked out for me very well since my wife dumped me. So I'm uneasy about relationships."

"Oh," she answered, her voice softening, thinking that must have been really difficult for him to say. No wonder he was using the telephone instead of speaking face-to-face.

"We started off on the wrong foot," he said. "I was focused on my job."

"You're supposed to be focused on your job," she

said, finding herself defending him. "I told you, I don't hold it against you."

"What about the kiss?"

"I liked the kiss," she whispered, because one thing she knew, being dishonest now would be a disaster.

"Good, because I can't stop fantasizing about what I'd like to do with you."

Her breath caught. "What?"

"You know, don't you?"

"Tell me."

"If I do, will you get angry about it?

"No. I want to know," she murmured.

She heard him drag in a breath and let it out slowly. "Okay. If you want to know, I'd like to come in there and take your clothes off. I want to lay you on the bed, naked. I want to look at you, then kiss you and touch you and make you as hot as I am now."

"Oh!"

"Am I turning you on?" he asked.

6

AMANDA SWALLOWED. The cautious woman she had been for so long told her she should halt this conversation right now.

But she didn't want to. The first time Zachary Grant had knocked on the door, she'd been in the bedroom alone—and close to orgasm. She'd been hot and bothered ever since then, and he had just turned up the heat.

"Yes," she breathed.

"Good."

"What about you? Is this making you...aroused?"

He laughed softly. "What do you think?"

"What are we going to do about it?" she heard herself ask. Lord, she'd never been this forward with a guy in her life. If she ended up in a sexual relationship, it was because the guy went after her.

She wasn't prepared for his next words. "I'm going to show you how much pleasure we can give each other—over the phone."

She turned her head toward the hall. He was only a few yards from her. Was she really going to engage in activities that she wasn't sure about? What she heard herself say was, "Let me close the bedroom door."

"Okay."

Her legs weren't entirely steady as she made it to

the door then back to the bed where she threw herself down with a little exclamation.

Maybe he heard it because he said, "You are so damn sexy."

"Am I?"

"Oh, yes. You're a very potent combination."

"Of?"

"Very beautiful woman and no-nonsense professional. I was intimidated by you, you know."

"Why?"

"Because you write that column. Then when you opened the door, you looked like a vision out of my dreams. Only you were real—standing right there in front of me. You're so much prettier than that publicity photo Beth gave me."

"When I opened the door, I had been thinking about you," she heard herself say, then could have bitten back the revealing comment.

There was a long pause on the other end of the line. "You hadn't met me," he said carefully.

"No, but Beth had left a message on my answering machine telling me you were…coming."

"Oh yeah?"

"You know what I mean."

"Mm-hmm."

"She told me about you. She described you…" She let her voice trail off.

"What did she say?"

"Now who's fishing for compliments?"

He laughed again. She loved that laugh. It was yummy. Like hot fudge on vanilla ice cream. But she wasn't going to make another mistake and tell him that.

He was right. Talking on the phone unleashed her

inhibitions in a way she might have found shocking, if she'd had time to be shocked.

"Are you wearing the T-shirt and shorts you put on after I left this morning?" he asked suddenly.

"Yes. Why?"

"I want to picture you as accurately as I can. You said you were aroused. Are your nipples standing up? If I were there in the bedroom with you, could I see them through your T-shirt?"

"T-shirt and bra!" She looked down and saw the twin points outlined by the soft fabric. The bra did nothing to hide them. She had taken her lower lip between her teeth when he said, "Are they nice hard little points?"

She breathed out a little sigh. "Yes."

"So take your hands and just run them over those tips. Do that for me."

This was crazy. She should stop. But she knew she didn't want to stop. So she did as he asked and made a small sound of pleasure.

"Ah, that's nice," he murmured. "Did you do that with the fronts of your fingers—or the backs?"

"The backs," she told him, hearing the catch in her voice, fighting embarrassment.

He didn't give her time for embarrassment. "Where are you?" he asked quickly.

"Lying down."

"Are your legs together? Or spread apart?"

"Together," she whispered. Pressing them together was increasing her arousal.

"Open them for me."

"Why?"

"I want to picture you that way. Spread open for me."

"Oh!" She did as he asked and found that it made her even hotter to follow his directions.

"If I were there with you, I'd run my hands up the insides of your legs, up your thighs and find the nice, hot center of you. Would that feel good?"

She couldn't answer—only make a strangled exclamation.

"Are you wet for me?"

This time, against all odds, she managed to get out one syllable. "Yes." But she was glad that he couldn't see the red flush heating her cheeks.

She was feeling like a blushing schoolgirl. Because she wanted to take back some control, she asked, "Are you still on the couch? I want to picture where you are."

"Yeah, I'm lying down now."

"Did you take off your shoes?"

He laughed. "Worried about the furniture?"

"No. I want you to be comfortable."

"Do you?"

"Yes," she whispered, then went a daring step further. "Very comfortable."

"Well I am."

The sound of his voice seemed to flow around her—warm and rich.

She liked it a lot. But she could still hang up, she told herself. She *should* hang up, because there was something distinctly indecent about this very intimate conversation conducted over the phone—with a man who was just down the hall. Any woman with high moral standards would gently set the receiver into the cradle and get back to real life.

She would have told one of her readers that this activity was only a fantasy, a substitute for reality, and was no way to get into a relationship with a man she barely knew. But it felt real, so she didn't take her own advice. Instead she gathered up her courage and said, "Are you hard?"

Amanda hardly breathed as she waited for Zachary's answer. He had turned her on, and she needed to know that she was doing the same thing to him. Well, that wasn't exactly true. She was sure he was aroused. But that wasn't enough. She was sharing very intimate details with him, and she needed to hear him give her the same kind of trust. Otherwise, she'd know she was making a bad mistake.

"You know I'm hard," he said, his voice thick.

She liked the way he said it, as though he were having trouble catching his breath.

"So if you can ask me to touch my breasts, can I ask you to press your hand against…against your penis."

"Oh yeah. You can do that."

She knew from his indrawn breath that he'd followed her directions.

"Rock your hand back and forth," she said. "The way I would if I were there," she added, shocked that she'd gotten the sentence out. But what he'd told her had been correct. She could say things on the phone that she wouldn't have been able to say in person.

As she closed her eyes, picturing him lying on the couch, his hand moving over the front of his jeans, she felt her own arousal leap higher.

"Did you like telling me what to do?" he asked, his voice silky but not quite steady.

"Yes."

"Um. Good. Then it's my turn. Take off your shirt

and your bra," he murmured. "Take them off for me."

She closed her eyes, thinking that never in her wildest imaginings would she have thought she could do any of this in a phone conversation.

There was still time to back out. She could stop this any time she wanted. He wasn't forcing her into anything. Maybe that was why she put down the receiver so she could pull her shirt over her head. Then she unhooked her bra and tossed it onto the spread beside her before picking up the phone again.

"Did you do it?" he asked, his tone warm and sultry in her ear.

"Yes."

"I know the shape of your breasts. I saw them last night."

"I wasn't expecting company."

"I know. And I appreciated the view. Your breasts aren't too large. But they're very nicely rounded. Just right for my hands."

"Ah…"

"What color are your nipples?" he suddenly asked.

"I…"

He spoke low, urgent words in her ear. "Sweetheart, don't keep anything back from me, I'm greedy. I want everything you're willing to give me."

"I…" she started again. "Peach? I don't know. I never thought about it."

"Peach. That sounds so pretty. Are they very sensitive?"

She swallowed. "Yes."

"So tell me what feels good."

"Please, Zachary, I can't."

"Of course you can. Don't you advise your readers to communicate with their partners?"

"Yes."

"So what would you like me to do to those pretty peach nipples? Circle each of them with one finger? Would that make them harder? Tighter? Needier?"

She answered with a little moan.

"Now that they're harder, do you want me to take them between my thumbs and fingers? Pull on them? Squeeze? How hard should I squeeze?"

"Some…" she managed to say.

"Do it for me."

She couldn't help herself now. Wedging the phone between her ear and her shoulder, she used both hands to play with her nipples, touching them lightly, then harder, her breath coming faster as her arousal built.

"Oh yeah, sweetheart. Oh yeah, that's good, so good."

"Zachary, I need…" She broke off, embarrassed.

"It's all right to tell me. We're communicating with each other. Do you want to come? Do you need to come?"

"Yes," the syllable hissed out of her.

"Kick off your shorts and panties for me. Do that for me."

Arousal had taken over her body and her mind. She was so desperate now that she did as he asked.

"Touch yourself for me. Down there, between your legs. You're hot and wet, aren't you? Stroke your finger through those sweet folds for me. If I were there, I'd find out what you like. Would you like me to dip my finger into your vagina? Just barely around the rim where you're so very sensitive. Or deeper.

Should I use one finger, or would two be better? How do you want me to do it?"

She couldn't answer. His description of what he could do to her was making her breath come in jagged gasps, and she knew she was close to climax.

"Do it for me."

Helpless to disobey, she reached down with her own hand, finding the hot, swollen core of herself, pressing and stroking.

"How do you like it? Long, slow strokes? From your vagina to your clit? Do that for me."

Her breath came in little pants. But there was something she had to say. "You, too," she gasped. "I can't do this unless you do it...too."

"Oh yeah, baby, I'm right here with you. All the way."

She heard the truth of his words in the uneven sound of his voice, in the ragged breaths that came over the phone line.

She pictured him lying on the couch, his fly unzipped, his penis standing up red and hard as his hand moved up and down the shaft, propelling himself toward climax.

Her own fingers were busy, making her body vibrate like a tuning fork, the pleasure building to flash point.

"Amanda," he gasped out, just as orgasm took her over the edge, and she moaned into the phone receiver that was still clamped between her ear and her shoulder.

She lay there for long seconds, breathing hard, little ripples of pleasure still tingling through her.

It took several moments before she drifted back to earth. But when she finally felt the firmness of the mattress beneath her shoulders, reality slammed back into her.

Zachary was out there in the living room. And she wondered how in the world she was ever going to face him now.

"Amanda," he murmured, as if he knew exactly where her thoughts had landed now that the fires sweeping across her body had been put out.

"What?" she asked, knowing that the question had come out high and sharp as she reached for the shorts and panties she'd discarded and dragged them on.

"Don't be embarrassed."

"Why not?" She fumbled across the bed for her T-shirt and bra. Transferring the phone from one hand to the other, she quickly got herself dressed again— because she was going to make damn sure that he didn't come down the hall and find her naked.

Her head swung to the door. He wouldn't come in here? Not now, when she was feeling totally exposed and vulnerable.

Never in her life would she have imagined making herself come when someone else knew what she was doing. And certainly not with a man who was right in the same house with her.

"Are you okay?" he asked.

"Yes," she snapped.

"Amanda, that was very, very pleasurable—for both of us."

When she didn't answer, he pressed, "Wasn't it?"

Honesty made her answer, "Yes."

"Then there's nothing to be embarrassed about. You'd tell that to your readers, wouldn't you? That what we just did is only another expression of your sexuality. Of our relationship."

She laughed. "Who's the advice columnist here?"

"You are. And now you have a better understanding of a very…stimulating aspect of male/female sexuality."

She closed her eyes, letting the words and the soft tone of his voice sink in. "Okay."

"I'm going to hang up now."

Her eyes blinked open. She wanted to shout, "no," because the phone had become a necessary extension of her body—a connection to Zachary. But the connection snapped, and she lay back against the bed. Reaching over she replaced the receiver on the cradle.

She'd wanted him to keep talking, wanted him to convince her that he didn't think less of her after what they'd just done. Now, she stared at a crack in the ceiling, thinking that it would be impossible to face the man in the living room.

She still had his phone number. Maybe she should just call him up and ask him to leave. That idea had some appeal. But it made her angry with herself. She was no coward, and she wasn't going to take the easy way out here.

She hadn't been the only one who reached orgasm a few minutes ago. Zachary had done it, too. And if she asked him to leave, she would never find out what that extraordinary phone call had meant to him.

Was he just having some fun with her? It certainly hadn't sounded that way. It had sounded like he'd been totally involved in what they were doing. It sounded like he'd enjoyed himself as much as she had. But she knew from personal experience that men were perfectly capable of taking advantage of women.

She thought about Bob Burns and squeezed her hands into fists. He'd started off making her trust him, and then he'd used his intimate knowledge of her to start rumors about her on campus.

He'd used her, and she hadn't even known what was happening until it was too late. Could Zachary Grant be the same kind of guy?

She didn't think so. But there was no way to be sure—except by getting to know him better. And he'd just made that a whole lot harder.

On the other hand, she knew he was inviting her to come out of the bedroom when the rich aroma of fresh-brewed coffee drifted down the hall and wafted under the door.

She dragged in a deep breath. He'd put on a pot of some blend that smelled very, very good.

Getting up, she walked stiffly to the bathroom and ran a comb through her hair. Telling herself she couldn't hide forever, she walked slowly down the hall to the kitchen.

Apparently he'd stopped to do some shopping. The coffee machine on the counter was almost full of dark liquid. Beside the pot sat a mug, a bottle of caramel syrup and a carton of heavy cream.

ZACHARY SAT at the kitchen table, trying to look relaxed. He had his back to the living room, but he'd heard Amanda moving around in the back of the house. And now she was walking slowly down the hall as though she were being invited to her own execution.

He knew she was nervous about facing him. And he wasn't any more calm, cool and collected about their phone session than she was.

When he heard her bare footsteps on the living

room floor, he stiffened, then made a concerted effort not to show the tension in his shoulders.

As far as he was concerned, what had happened a few minutes ago was a small miracle. But he couldn't tell her that. Not yet. Maybe never.

He wanted to shout, *say something, Amanda.* But he kept his lips pressed together as she walked directly to the counter, poured coffee into the mug he'd set out, then added cream and caramel syrup.

It took all his resolve to keep from jumping up and crossing the room, grabbing her by the shoulders and turning her toward him. But he stayed where he was, gripping his own ceramic mug, feeling the warmth from the fresh brew seep into his hands.

Eons passed. Finally he heard her clear her throat. "How did you know I like caramel in my coffee?"

"I didn't. But I saw the bottle, and I thought about how good it would taste."

She turned to face him, her expression uncertain.

Are you going to throw me out? The question stayed locked inside his mind. To moisten his dry throat, he took another sip of the coffee. He'd picked the blend because it sounded good. Maybe it really was good, but he couldn't taste it.

Amanda took a sip of coffee. Then another.

Setting her mug on the table, she started to sit. Which gave him the opportunity he'd been waiting for.

As soon as there was no danger of her spilling the hot coffee, he was out of his chair and around the table.

Unable to say what he was feeling, he swept her into his arms, lowered his mouth and kissed her, try-

ing to put all the warmth and passion he possessed
into the kiss.

The last time had been an exploration. This kiss
was more desperate and more possessive. But he
broke it off long before he wanted to stop.

He lifted his lips from hers and skimmed them
along her cheek.

"Thank you," he murmured, his hand stroking
over her shoulders, then inching upward to tangle in
her hair.

"For what?" she whispered.

"For being willing to try something...different."
He swallowed around the tightness in his throat.
"Probably you're thinking I fool around like that all
the time. But it's not true. I've never come close to
anything like that before."

"Why did you start it—now?"

He swallowed again, figuring he had to be honest.
Well, at least as honest as he could be. "After I read
that letter on your desk, I couldn't stop thinking about
it." He managed a laugh. "I was going to seduce you
first—with the coffee and the cream and the caramel
syrup. Then slowly work my way around to suggesting we try the phone. Then I came home, and you
were in the bedroom, and I just...I just took a chance
and dialed your number. Are you angry about that?"

"No." Her throat worked. "I guess if you want to
know the truth...I'm embarrassed."

"Why?"

She could have ducked away from him. But he'd
learned that she wasn't the kind of woman who
avoided a subject because it made her uncomfortable.
"Because touching yourself is a very personal thing.
I did it with you on the other end of the phone line."

"Did you like it?"

A flush spread across her cheeks. "Yes."

"Good. Because I did, too." He paused and dragged in a breath. "I did some reading about sexual therapy...before I came down here to interview you." A long time before, but he didn't voice the qualification. "One thing I read was that the more comfortable partners are in letting the other person know what they want, the better their relationship will be."

She nodded.

"So that's what we did."

She sighed, as though she weren't quite certain. And he figured that it might be time for a change of subject. How about from sex to stalkers?

"We should go back to your old house to get your things."

"Oh, right. I wasn't thinking about that."

"After we finish our coffee."

When she pulled out her chair and sat down, some of the tightness in his chest eased.

"And I should question you some more."

Her head jerked up. "About what?"

"Did you think about who might want to hurt you? Did you have a fight with anyone recently?"

She turned her coffee mug in her hands. "You want me to dredge up every little thing? A few days ago at the grocery store a man and I both wanted the same space, and he shook his fist at me."

"Was he driving a white van?"

"No."

"We can assume that was an isolated occurrence."

"Okay, I had an...incident with a guy who lives near that other house. I went out on his boat dock to look at the river, and he came down there and yelled at me for trespassing. Then a few other times when I passed him on the road, he glared at me.''

''I'll have a chat with him.''

''You will?''

''Yeah. You can point out his property when I stop by there.'' He leaned back in his seat and stretched out his legs. She'd named two minor incidents, but she'd omitted someone from her past. Did she trust him enough to talk about what had happened before she'd moved down here?

She looked down, turning her coffee cup again. ''Something happened at Harmons College.''

''Oh?'' he asked, his breath shallow.

Her cheeks had taken on a deepened color. ''I was accused of getting too…friendly with some of my male students.''

''*Were* you too friendly with them?''

''No! I'm not interested in relationships with college boys. But some of them were interested in me.''

''I can understand why.''

''Thanks—I think.''

''You're beautiful. You're sexy. You were a target because you taught classes on human sexuality. I bet a lot of guys had fantasies about you.''

''I know all that.'' She dragged in a breath and let it out. ''Unfortunately, there were rumors about me. That's what made me take a leave of absence.''

He nodded.

''The rumors were started by another professor, Bob Burns. He was new at the school. He went out of his way to be friendly to me. We…we got into a relationship. Then I found out he'd set his sights on being head of the department—a job I was in line for.''

"Nice guy."

"I thought he was. I found out he manipulated people to get what he wanted."

"Why would he come after you down here?"

"He worked hard to get me out of the picture. He might want to make sure I stay away from Harmons."

"Would you go back?"

She hesitated. "I inherited some money from my mother. It's enough to live on—modestly—for a few years. I was hoping that I could establish myself as a writer. The column should help with that. Then I won't have to worry about teaching."

"You don't like teaching?"

"Actually, I do. But there are times when I want to focus on my own work. So I'd like to be able to take on a reduced class load."

"I thought Esther Scott's identity has to remain secret. How can the column help you in a writing career?"

"For now, it's got to be secret. But I'm hoping to give the column a different tone. And if I'm successful, *Vanessa* might want to promote me."

"How would you make the column different?"

"Sometimes it sounded like Esther didn't respect the people who wrote letters. At least it felt to me like she was using them to get a laugh."

"Yeah."

"You read the column?"

"Sure. I want to know as much about her as possible."

"And what did you find out?"

"I wouldn't have liked her very much." He pushed back his chair. "Come on, we need to get over to your old house. How long were you there?"

"A little over a month."

"And it was furnished. So there won't be a lot to move."

"Food. My clothing. Sheets and towels. A few other things."

"I wish you didn't have to go back there. I could handle it for you."

She looked uncomfortable. "I don't really love the idea of your handling my underwear. So let's do it together."

Underwear? Or something else she didn't want him to know about? He was trained to catch the subtle changes in a person's voice. The remark had sounded innocent, but she'd let him know by the tone of her voice that she was holding something back, and he was going to find out what it was.

Could he do that without wrecking their relationship? He sure as hell hoped so.

Because it would kill him now if he found out something underhanded about her.

7

AMANDA SETTLED into the front seat of Zachary's Honda. If she weren't so uncomfortable about going back to her former rented house to pack, it would be a pleasure to watch him do his P.I. thing.

She might have questioned his methods that first afternoon. But as she sat beside him now, there was no doubt that he was a professional. He took a roundabout route to the old house, being careful to make sure that no other vehicle was staying in back of them. And he was especially careful as he approached the street where she'd lived—looking for cars or vans that seemed suspicious, she supposed.

After circling the area for ten minutes, he declared that they were, "All clear."

She was still wondering how she was going to get the vibrator into her luggage without him seeing it.

She hated that her mind was focused on the damn tool. She knew her anxiety was a reflection of her personality. A more assertive woman would stride into the bedroom, pull it out of the drawer and simply pack it with her other personal items. There was nothing wrong with having a vibrator. Nothing at all.

But Amanda couldn't help thinking about what her mother would say. And she knew that despite the fact that she'd answered the reader's question on masturbation with a very positive pep talk, she was obviously embarrassed about admitting that she engaged in that activity herself. Or—to be more specific—embarrassed to let a guy she found attractive know she had a vibrator. He pulled the Honda to a stop in the driveway as close as he could to the kitchen door. They both got out, and she fumbled with the key, conscious that he was watching her as he unloaded cardboard boxes from the trunk.

She could see he was trying to appear casual. But she was very aware of the assessing look in his eyes. It was the look she remembered from that first afternoon when he'd asked to use the bathroom—when his real intent was to search her room.

So, what was he thinking?

Again, she knew that another woman would come out and ask that question—making it a challenge. She simply said, "I'm a little nervous about being here. I mean after that guy breaking in last night."

"I understand."

She unlocked the door, and they both stepped into the kitchen, standing awkwardly in the middle of the tile floor. At least she was feeling awkward.

When she realized he was speaking, she forced herself to focus on his words. "We want to get out of here as quickly as we can," he said.

He'd given her the perfect opening. "Could you clear the shelves in the linen closet? All the towels and sheets are mine. And I'll pack up the bedroom. Also, the cleaning supplies under the kitchen sink."

"Good idea," he agreed.

She showed him the linen closet, then hurried to the bedroom. First she filled a box with underwear and other clothing. Then, after a quick glance over her shoulder, she hurried over to the bedside table.

Just as she slid the drawer open, she heard footsteps rapidly cross the floor, and her body went rigid.

She breathed in Zachary's aftershave, then turned enough so that she could see him filling the doorway.

Apparently he'd been keeping tabs on her, and she hadn't even known it.

As she looked down into the drawer, she felt him glide up behind her.

"What is it that you're hiding in there?" he growled.

Unable to answer, she stood in front of the bedside table, keeping her eyes cast down, focused on the vibrator. There was absolute silence in the room now, and she was pretty sure she knew when he spotted the off-white plastic shaft because she heard him swallow hard.

Unwilling to turn and face him, she simply stood there. Long seconds ticked by before she finally broke the deafening silence with a question, "What did you think I was hiding—a stash of coke? Or maybe a cozy little letter from Esther's killer?"

"No."

"I know that look in your eye."

"You can't see my eyes."

"In the car. Your suspicious look. You thought I was up to something illegal."

"I thought I had a poker face."

"Maybe under ordinary circumstances. But I'm good at reading people."

"So am I. There's nothing wrong with using a vibrator."

"You don't have to tell me that!" she snapped. "It's a perfectly legitimate...toy for a woman to have. I would certainly tell that to readers. I just happen to be embarrassed about being seen with one in my bed-side table drawer. And I was hoping I'd have some privacy when I packed it.''

"Yeah."

She dragged in a breath and let it out, wishing he'd back away from her. At the moment, she wanted to be alone.

"I didn't intend to embarrass you."

"Is that an apology?"

"Yes." He hesitated for a moment, then added, "Part of doing my job is judging your moods."

"Oh, that's just great."

"That's why I followed you into the bedroom."

"And now you can stop snooping."

"I'm not trying to make life difficult for you."

With any other man, she would have said, "Why don't you just let me finish packing. Then you can take me back to my new rental property and go back to New York." That's what she should say, she told herself. But Zachary Grant wasn't just any man. He was a man who had gotten very close to her in a very short period of time.

That was dangerous in itself. But it also presented an opportunity.

OUTSIDE ON THE STREET, Tony Anderson slowed the white van and stared at the Honda parked in the drive-way. In the next moment, he speeded up.

The Honda had been there the day before. It belonged to the guy he had started to call Mr. Buttinski. The guy who had been hanging around Amanda O'Neal. The guy who had almost coldcocked him.

So the bastard was back. Or the two of them were

there. Good—unless one of them picked this exact moment to come outside.

Tony speeded up again, drove down the rural road, and turned off into a long driveway, screened by trees from the road. Then he got out a map and pretended that he was trying to find a particular address.

Really, he was thinking about what to do now. He'd been circling back here every half hour or so, hoping to spot O'Neal. She'd been gone since the incident last night. But she'd left her car at the house. So he'd figured she was coming back. He'd hoped to catch her alone. But it looked like Buttinski was back, too.

The guy was dangerous. Tony had barely gotten away last night. So he was going to be damn careful not to get caught now.

But he couldn't simply leave, because this was too good an opportunity.

If O'Neal came out, he'd follow her. Or if the guy left, that might give him another crack at the woman. Either way, he felt like his luck had turned again.

WHILE SHE WAS TRYING to decide what to say and what to do, Amanda felt Zachary move in closer behind her so that the front of his body was pressed to the back of hers.

His voice had turned low and intimate when he said, ''The most important thing I want you to understand is that I find the contents of your bedside table very sexy.''

''Why?'' she managed to say, her own voice cracking on the single syllable.

''Because it tells me that your sexuality is important to you. You don't deny that component of your personality. You make a point of keeping in touch with the sensual side of your nature.''

''Oh.''

Apparently her ability to speak had been reduced to monosyllables. And all hope of speech choked off completely when he leaned over, reached into the drawer and picked up the vibrator. She wanted to close her eyes, but her gaze was riveted to the eight-inch-long plastic shaft grasped in his hand.

It looked so out of place in his large fist. But when he ran his thumb up the length of the thing, a low, buzzing sound started up in her head, making it almost impossible to string one thought after the other. She assumed it was the pounding of the blood in her veins. Then she realized he had switched on the motor.

''I never used one of these things,'' he murmured. ''It makes your skin tingle—just holding it in your hand.''

''Um.'' He was making *her* skin tingle. And she knew she wasn't the only one affected because she now felt the unmistakable shaft of an erection pressing against her bottom.

They were standing beside the bed, and she felt trapped between his body and the edge of the mattress. She could step around him and leave the room. But she had the feeling her legs wouldn't carry her across the carpet now. When she swayed on her feet, he crossed his free arm over her chest, pulling her back so that most of her weight rested against him.

''You should let me go,'' she breathed.

''Why?''

''It's...''

''Very arousing,'' Zach finished the sentence for

her. Then he dipped his head, kissing the side of her neck, the edge of her jaw, loving the feel of her silky skin against his lips.

He couldn't believe he was holding her like this, doing the things he was doing, but there was no way he could stop himself now—not unless she pushed him away.

And he had to give her that chance, because he didn't want either one of them to think he was forcing her into anything. So he ordered himself to loosen his hold on her. When she stayed where she was, he breathed out a small sigh.

Slowly, deliberately, he moved his other hand, the one that held the vibrator.

"I've seen ads for these things in magazines. In the ads, they always show the shaft against the woman's cheek," he said, stroking the plastic shaft against that very part of her anatomy, then her neck.

The low buzz of the plastic wand so close to his own head had set off a muzzy sensation in his brain. Probably anything he did now would set his head spinning.

He shifted his other arm so he could move the plastic wand lower, playing it over her breasts, over their hard, distended tips.

The small gasp that escaped from her lips was like a jolt of electricity through his own body.

Closing his eyes, he nibbled at the edge of her cheek. "You are so, so sexy," he murmured, "so responsive." He opened his eyes again, looking down at her breasts, liking his vantage point. "When we were talking on the phone, I was picturing how you looked. I wanted to touch you so badly."

He played the vibrator across those nicely rounded

swells for another moment, then eased away just far enough so that he could reach under the back of her knit top and unhook the snap of her bra. One-handed. *Very proficient, Grant,* he thought, with a satisfied grin.

He felt her breathing accelerate as he shifted his free hand to the front of her again, then pushed her top up, taking the bra with it, bunching the fabric around her neck and shoulders. He drew in a quick, sharp breath as he looked down at her breasts, following the creamy curves to the their tight, hard centers. The color looked darker than peach to him, probably because of the increased blood supply.

The vibrator was an extension of his hand as he used it to circle those hard tips, first one, and then the other, feeling her arch into the caress.

He wanted to taste her. But he couldn't do it now, because that would violate the rules of the game he was making up as he went along.

He kept the vibrating wand on one nipple, then used his free hand to play with its mate, loving the feel of her puckered flesh between his fingers.

"Oh…"

"You like that?"

"Yes," she gasped out.

He liked it, too. Very much. But it wasn't enough. Not hardly.

The waistband of her shorts was elastic—made for easy removal. He kept the vibrator at breast level but slid his free hand down her body, pausing to caress the expanse of skin below her breasts before flattening his hand and sliding his fingers under the elastic of her shorts.

It pulled away easily, permitting him comfortable access to the treasures hidden by the garment.

She moaned and wiggled against him, pressing her bottom against his rigid cock. He swallowed a gasp of pleasure.

He itched to tear off her clothing, strip her naked. But the part of his brain still functioning suspected that might be going too far, under the circumstances. So he contented himself with slipping his hand farther under the fabric, combing his trembling fingers through the springy hair at the juncture of her legs, then dipping lower, into the hot swollen folds of her most intimate flesh.

When he pulled his hand away, she whimpered in protest—he hoped because now she needed him to do something about the fire he'd kindled in her blood.

"I'm not going anywhere," he murmured, his lips nibbling at her ear as he reversed the position of his hands, sliding the vibrator down her body, while his free hand came up to play with one breast.

He had never used a vibrator on a woman, but he was pretty sure the tingling sensation he felt in his fingers would be even more effective on her clit. "Do you put this thing inside you?" he asked.

"Not usually. I…"

"I think I can figure it out," he whispered. He held the magic wand vertically against her clit, rocking it slightly, feeling her squirm in his grasp. He felt her heart pounding under his other hand, heard her breath hissing in and out of her lungs. She threw her head back against his shoulder, and he could see her eyes were squeezed shut. Then her whole body went rigid and she cried out with the force of her orgasm. He kept the vibrator where it was until she slumped back against him, knowing that the orgasm would be better if he continued giving her stimulation until she was finished.

When he felt her relax, he pulled the penis-shaped device out of her shorts and switched off the motor, but his hand still grasped the hard plastic as he tried to bring his own reactions under control.

"Zachary?"

Her question brought his mind back into focus.

"I think you know me well enough to call me Zach," he said, brushing his lips against the top of her hair.

"Zach," she repeated in an unsteady voice. "I…" She didn't finish the sentence. She still stood with her face away from him. But her head was bent, and he knew that now that she'd come back to earth, she was probably abashed by what had just happened. He wanted to get the damn vibrator out of his hand. Tossing it on the bed would be sort of crass, he thought. So he set it quietly down on the bedside table.

Then he skimmed his lips against her jawline as he reached to pull her bra down and her shirt back into place. He thought about hooking the bra, then decided he should leave that for her.

Still nuzzling her neck and the side of her face, he whispered, "That was incredible."

She cleared her throat and tried to turn, but he held her where she was. "What about you?" she asked, her voice very husky and very sexy.

"I'm fine," he answered quickly.

"You're…" She reached around behind her, and he was sure she was trying to force the issue. Which he wasn't going to allow. Instead, he took a quick step back, catching the hand that was headed for his cock.

"We'll worry about me later."

"I'm not in the habit of...of taking my pleasure and not giving anything back."

He thought about telling her that being in this condition was all too familiar for him, then decided he'd be a fool to open himself up to that extent.

But he needed a reason why they weren't going to be doing anything else right now. The answer came to him in a flash, and he felt a surge of embarrassment of his own. When he swore under his breath, she turned her head to look at him.

"What?"

"We came here to get your clothing because you were being stalked by the guy who broke in here last night. We were going to get in and out of the house as fast as we could so he wouldn't get another crack at you. Fooling around wasn't on the schedule."

"I wasn't planning to fool around," she murmured.

He made his voice soothing. "I know that. What happened was entirely my fault. Well—let's not think of it in terms a felony. I saw a very sexy opportunity and I took it. But now we're going to get back on track. Collect your stuff so we can leave."

ZACH EXITED the room, leaving Amanda still standing by the bed. Glad to be alone again, Amanda quickly fit her breasts back into the cups of the bra, adjusted the straps, then worked the hook at the back.

Breathing out a little sigh, she looked around the room. The vibrator was lying on the bedside table. Snatching it up, she shoved it into the box of clothing that she'd emptied from the drawers. Then she went into the bathroom where she started putting toilet articles into another box.

At first she was glad to let the activity occupy her mind. Then she found herself thinking about Zachary. Zach.

He'd made love to her as they stood beside the bed. Well, not exactly making love. But he'd touched her and kissed her and brought her to climax with the hard shaft of the vibrator—after he'd told her that finding the damn thing in her drawer was sexy. He'd given her great pleasure, and she'd been prepared to return the favor any way he wanted. Before she could, he'd backed away.

She didn't think many guys would have gone that route. So what was Zach Grant thinking—really?

He'd come up with the perfect excuse. In fact, she understood that they had to get out of here. But she was willing to bet that he'd cited the danger because he didn't want the physical stuff to focus on him.

Why not?

Did she know him well enough to ask him?

And what would he say? Either the man was very good at manipulation, or he was hiding something about his personality—something that they should bring out into the light.

She glanced toward the bed, then remembered what had happened the night before. He'd been in the grip of a nightmare, and she'd tried to help. He'd awakened and assumed she was his enemy. He'd been upset about that. Maybe he was still upset. Maybe he was thinking that he didn't trust himself in bed with her again.

If that was the problem, they could work on it together. But this was the wrong time and the wrong place.

So she finished packing her toilet articles and makeup, then returned to the bedroom. After stripping the bed, she folded up the bottom sheet and comforter into a pillowcase. Then she used the top sheet as a makeshift garment bag for the clothing hanging in the closet—which reminded her to get her luggage from the front hall closet.

When she returned to the living room, she found that Zach had put her books and magazines into boxes.

He was carefully wrapping a vase in newspaper, which he set into a box with other wrapped objects.

"What else?" he asked, keeping his voice very matter of fact. And she knew he was hoping she would stay focused on the packing.

She decided not to disappoint him. And when she started removing the few knickknacks she'd brought from Annapolis, she saw him let out a little sigh.

Then she started opening kitchen cabinets and drawers. Most of the dishes and other equipment had come with the house. But there were a few things she'd brought with her—like some of her favorite coffee mugs.

"I think we just have to load up the food," she said.

"I'll take the refrigerator. You do the cabinet," he suggested.

"Thanks."

They worked together efficiently, and in less than ten minutes everything was ready to go.

When they both carried the boxes to the Honda, Zach looked from the vehicle to her car, a considering expression on his face. She'd come to know that expression very well.

"What's wrong?"

"I'm trying to figure out how to get you home safely." He glanced up and down the street. "Somebody could be watching to see where we end up after we leave here, so I'm going to take a roundabout way back to your new place. I want you to do the same. Take a circuitous route—and watch your rearview mirror. But don't go home. Drive to the shopping center that's about a mile from your new house. We passed it, remember?"

"Yes."

"When you get there, find a space near the entrance to the grocery store where you're visible to a lot of people. Make sure your doors are locked, and wait for me there."

"Is all that necessary?" she asked.

"I think it is. You have your cell phone?"

She reached into her purse and found it. "Yes."

"Call me immediately if you see anything suspicious."

FROM BEHIND A SCREEN of trees fifty yards away, Tony watched them standing in the driveway. It sounded like Mr. Buttinski was giving her directions, laying out what they were going to do.

The Honda pulled out of the driveway and O'Neal followed in her car, both of them turning in the direction away from where he watched.

Buttinski wouldn't want anyone to know where they were going. He probably had something tricky in mind, like sending both of them on a long, winding route that would be hard to follow. No doubt about it, the guy was primed for trouble, expecting anyone staking out the place to follow O'Neal.

Was that his best choice? Or should he go with the guy?

He didn't like this damn complication. If Buttinski hadn't appeared on the scene, he'd have Amanda O'Neal in his power already. That's where he wanted her. Because she'd taken over that damn column from Esther Knight.

As he thought about his plans for her, he felt himself growing hard. It hadn't started out as sexual—when he'd killed Esther Knight a couple of months ago. But he'd been pleasantly surprised by the sexual jolt he'd gotten out of slamming that car into her.

He'd liked the feeling, and he'd realized that he'd shortchanged himself by being so impersonal. She'd been on the street. He'd been in the car. And the thrill of wiping her off the face of the earth had been over much too quickly. But he wasn't going to make that mistake with Amanda O'Neal. The two of them were going to spend some quality time together. Get to know each other. He was looking forward to it. Very much. Because any woman who thought she could step into Esther Scott's shoes deserved anything she got.

8

DEAR ESTHER,

I met a man whom I can't figure out. I mean, I
like him and I think he likes me. I haven't known
him long. But so far, he's constantly surprising
me. Well, sometimes surprises that make me uncomfortable, actually. There are times I'm sure
he doesn't trust me. Other times, I'm certain he
wants to protect me. He's very complicated. And
our sexual relationship is complicated, too. I've
done things with him that I've never done with
anyone else—things that might embarrass me
with another man. But he makes it seem fine.
Well, except that I blush when I think how far
I've gone with him in such a short time. What
do you think I ought to do? Ditch him? Or let
him help me explore my sexuality?

Amanda sat in her car, composing a letter in her
mind to occupy her thoughts while she peered out the
windshield, waiting for Zach to appear.

Let him? Was that the right phrase? Was she letting
him talk her into doing things that made her uncomfortable?

Once again, she wished there was somebody she
could consult. Not Esther Scott. One of her old friends

from Harmons. But she'd walked away from her support system. Well, walked away from the friends she'd had left. The rest of them had turned their backs on her.

For just a moment, she thought about calling her sister. Emily was a computer programmer living in California. But they'd never been close. And her sister had absorbed their parents' values. More than likely she'd be embarrassed if Amanda tried to ask for advice about her relationship with Zach.

She sighed. Was it a relationship? A sexual relationship?

Well, the first episode with him had been all talk. The second had been all hot touching and kissing.

Her hands clenched and unclenched as she fought to ward off the feelings that came along with the memories.

They had the power to arouse her. And arousal should be the furthest thing from her mind, now.

Instead, she tried to focus on Zach, the man. Their relationship was artificial. They'd been thrown together because he was a private detective investigating the murder of the woman who'd written the Esther Scott column. But he'd chosen to stay with her. Which must mean something. But she couldn't figure out what it was.

She craned her neck, looking first at one entrance to the parking lot—then the other. But she didn't see Zach.

She'd been here for twenty minutes, watching people go in and out of the store, seeing some of them eyeing her—probably wondering what she was doing sitting here all that time.

At first she'd been keyed up. Now she was worried, if she was going to admit the truth to herself.

She had expected Zach to meet her before this. Too bad she hadn't gone inside the store and done some grocery shopping. While she'd been sitting here, she had thought of several items she needed.

And she'd been thinking that if she bought some chicken or some sirloin steak, she could impress him with her chicken cacciatore or her beef stroganoff. She might not be a whiz in the kitchen, but over the years she'd collected a few good dishes that she could always rely on.

She made a small snorting sound. So now she was thinking about bowling him over with her cooking. Terrific!

She dragged her mind away from that topic. Then, unable to stop herself, she went back to worrying again. She could dial his number on the cell phone. But that would give away that she was on edge, and she didn't want to call him, because it was exactly what her mother would have done. Mom's specialty had been calling to find out why you hadn't arrived at the exact time she expected you. That trait had annoyed Amanda, which was why she'd vowed never to do it.

But this was completely different. Maybe it was time to break her own rules. She had just pulled out her cell phone when she saw Zach's Honda coming down the curb lane. Quickly she put it away.

He swung into the empty space beside her and rolled down his window.

"The coast is clear. You can follow me back."

"Okay," she answered. She'd been worried that Zach was somehow in danger because of her. Because of the murder investigation. The moment she saw him and knew that he was all right, she went back to worrying about their relationship.

She stayed in back of him as they returned to the new house he'd found for her, the whole process gobbling up fifteen minutes more than if they'd taken the direct route.

The property was on a large lot, with a deep backyard that faced the creek. Zach pulled up at the curb, then waved her around to the back, where her vehicle couldn't be seen from the street.

So she did as he asked, though she wasn't thrilled with all the cloak-and-dagger maneuvers.

When she glanced in the rearview mirror, she saw that he'd pulled his car to the end of the driveway, effectively blocking her exit from the property, and she fought a sudden trapped feeling that tightened her chest.

She told herself to calm down. He hadn't locked her in. He was simply protecting her. He was a former cop. Now he was a private detective. For him, watching his back at all times was as ingrained as brushing his teeth in the morning.

"I should have gone shopping," she said when she'd climbed out of her car.

"I was thinking that after we unload, we could go out to dinner."

"We can?" she asked. "I mean, I thought we had to hide."

"Basically, we have to stay off the beaten track. But I was considering our options. There are plenty of little restaurants in out-of-the-way corners of the county. One of them ought to be a safe place to have dinner."

"Okay. I'd like that."

"Work first. Play later," he said, his voice light. But as soon as the words were out of his mouth, she found herself thinking that they'd already been playing.

From the expression on his face, it looked like his thoughts were traveling in the same direction.

"Let's get unloaded," he said, then swung quickly back toward the Honda.

They both carried in her belongings, with Zach grabbing the heavier boxes. The job didn't take long because she'd used different containers for different areas of the house. Some went right to the bedroom or the bathroom while others could be left in the kitchen.

When she got to the vibrator, she hesitated, unable to put it into the drawer of the bedside table. When Zach came to bed with her, they'd both be thinking about it.

She stopped short, raising her hand and pressing her fingers to her mouth.

When he came to bed with her. In her thoughts, she'd used that phrase without a second's hesitation. Like she knew it was going to happen.

Well, if it didn't, she would be disappointed—and surprised. So far the things they'd done had been very stimulating. But she wanted to be in bed with him, his naked body clasped to hers. And it was hard to believe he didn't want that, too.

She canceled the graphic image as soon as it had formed in her mind. Better not to go any further down that path, because she was becoming aroused again. And it hadn't been that long since he'd brought her to a mind-blowing climax.

Unable to stop herself now, she stood for a moment with her eyes closed, reliving that intimate encounter with him. He knew how to touch a woman, knew how...

With a grimace, she looked toward the bedroom door as though she expected him to come striding down the hall. When he didn't, she picked up the pile of garments she'd laid on the bed and headed for the closet, making sure each was secure on its hanger.

Zach knocked on the door while she was still in the closet—with her back to him again.

Deliberately she turned around. "Come in."

He stopped in the doorway, as though he were thinking that if he came into the room, they'd end up tangled together on the bed. "I made a reservation at the Plantation," he said.

"The Plantation! Isn't that the most expensive restaurant around here?"

"Yeah, but I figure I can splurge."

"I don't expect you to pay for dinner!" she answered immediately.

"Well, I'm living here rent free. So don't feel bad about letting me take you out to a nice restaurant. The reservation is for seven, if that works for you."

"Yes. Thanks."

She spent much of the afternoon unpacking.

After Zach helped her with some of the heavier items, he told her he was going out and disappeared for a couple of hours.

While he was gone, she set up her computer on the desk in the bedroom, opened letters and read them.

Many of them would have made good jumping-off points for the column. But she found that her mind kept winging back to Zach.

Finally, she heard him come in and pushed back her chair, eager to find out where he'd been. Then she stopped herself. She was acting like a possessive wife, and that was hardly appropriate. Still, she was curious about why he'd been gone for hours.

When she came into the living room, she saw he was carrying a paper bag and a navy blue sports coat over his arm.

Seeing her eye the purchases, he said, "I didn't have anything to wear to the Plantation, so I bought something."

"We could have gone somewhere a lot less fancy," she answered.

"I know. But there's a good discount mall down here, and I decided to try one of the men's stores."

"That's where you were—at the mall?" she asked. "I thought men hated to shop."

His face took on an expression she couldn't quite read. "Sometimes it's a necessary evil."

"So was shopping the only thing you did?"

He shrugged. "We'll talk about it at dinner."

Feeling like a high school girl going out on an important date, she took a leisurely shower, fussed with her hair and makeup, then selected a cream-colored, summer weight pants outfit that she knew made her look taller and slimmer.

She accented the neckline with some onyx beads, slipped into white sandals, and studied the effect in the full-length mirror on the back of the closet door.

When she stepped into the living room, Zach was standing with his back to the room, gazing out at Turtle Creek. He turned—then stopped short, his gaze going warm as he inspected her outfit.

"Very nice," he murmured. "A very nice change from shorts and a T-shirt."

Some women might have bristled at the remark. But in fact, she'd gotten dressed up for him, and she was pleased that he liked the effect.

She liked the effect she was seeing as well. "You clean up pretty good yourself," she answered, because it was true. They'd only seen each other in the most casual of outfits. But his dark good looks were set off very nicely by the navy sports jacket, a white dress shirt, his chinos and a pair of brown loafers.

"Let's go," he said. When she'd climbed into the passenger seat of the car, he opened his door and stuck his head inside. "I forgot something in the house. Be right back," he said.

He went back in and returned quickly, looking like a little boy who'd been naughty and was hoping he wouldn't get caught.

He was up to something, but she wasn't going to ask what it was.

They didn't have much to say to each other on the way to the inn, and she began to wonder what they would talk about at dinner.

As he found a parking space in one of the shrubbery-screened lots near the inn, she turned to look at the building. She'd heard about the Plantation, of course. But she'd considered it out of her price range.

It had started life as an old manor house. But a series of additions had enlarged the building to accommodate overnight guests. There were also a number of guest houses dotted around the grounds.

In the front hall, a hostess confirmed their reservation, then led them to one of several dining rooms. Their table was by a window with a nice view of well-

tended gardens and a boat dock where several pleasure craft were moored. Apparently you could come
here by water if you were so inclined.

The table was set with crisp linen, flower patterned
china and gleaming cutlery.

"It's strange to find a place like this in a small,
out-of-the-way town," Amanda commented as they
took their seats.

"Well, the area has a very mixed economy. There
are the watermen and farmers whose families made
their living from the bay and the land for years. And
there are the wealthy people who have come down
here to escape from the city."

"You seem to know more about it than I do."

"Part of my research," he said.

They both looked up as a server approached the
table and asked, "Can I get you something to drink?"

Zach glanced at her. "How about some wine?"

Amanda was about to ask what they had by the
glass, when he requested the wine list.

She'd pegged him more as the beer type, but he
studied the leather-bound folder carefully, asked her
opinion, then ordered a merlot, which the waiter
brought to the table and uncorked.

"Where did you learn about wine?" she asked as
she sipped the dark, rich wine. It was excellent.

He laughed. "In college. I was a waiter. Part of the
job was being able to advise customers on wine. So
I tried a bunch of them and found I liked them."

"You know more about it than I do," she conceded. "A lot of times I just go for a white zinfandel."

"We used to say people who ordered zinfandel
didn't really like wine."

"I like it. I just don't know enough about it to feel comfortable."

"It's not that mysterious."

She wondered if he was going to be around long enough to give her wine-tasting lessons, then canceled the thought.

They ordered dinner, and she splurged on rack of lamb while he selected osso bucco.

"So how did you get interested in human sexuality?" he asked, when the waiter had departed again.

She took a sip of wine. "Isn't everybody?"

"Sure. But a lot of people just plunge right in. You made a study of the subject."

She shifted in her seat. Most people didn't ask her such direct questions. But most people weren't detectives, of course. She could be evasive, but she knew she wanted to be as open and honest with Zachary Grant as she could. "I guess my interest goes back to my parents. They were pretty repressed and repressive."

"Like how?"

Maybe it was the wine that made her answer, "One time I heard some older kids laughing and giggling about something—and I didn't know what it meant. So I asked my big sister, 'what does fuck mean?' She told my parents, and I got a spanking for saying that word."

"Nice."

She shrugged, knowing that the wine was lowering her inhibitions. "You know all kids wonder how their parents managed to have any children. It was true in spades for mine. I think now that after they had my sister and me, they stopped having sexual relations."

"That's pretty radical. I've heard about women

who never enjoyed making love and thought of all kinds of excuses to get out of it. Not many guys go that route.''

''I guess it wasn't very important to them.''

''So you wanted a different life.''

''Yes.''

''What about your sister?''

''She's still pretty uptight.''

''Is she married?''

''She was. It didn't work out.''

''Oh.''

''I don't think she liked sex. At least *I* didn't pick up that attitude from my parents,'' she heard herself saying defensively.

''But maybe your early experiences made you cautious about sexual experimentation.''

''Maybe,'' she conceded in a low voice.

He leaned back comfortably and crossed his legs at the ankles. ''I guess the column is broadening your horizons.''

''What do you mean?''

''You're finding out what other people do.''

She nodded.

''Do the letters inspire you to try new things?''

''I've only had this job for less than a month,'' she answered, thinking that she'd like to take the conversation in a less personal direction.

He sat forward and suddenly asked, ''Why didn't you absorb your parents' values?''

''I have a theory about kids. You either end up like your parents, or you do just the opposite.''

He looked thoughtful. ''I guess you're right.''

''You're speaking from personal experience.''

"Yeah. My dad was a very straight-arrow cop. I ended up in the same field. So did my brothers."

Feeling reckless, she said, "Straight-arrow. Did that mean your Dad wasn't into sex?"

"I think my parents had a very lusty relationship. I think they still do."

"Good for them."

An expression flashed across his face—something that she wasn't sure how to read.

"You said you have brothers. What about sisters?" she asked.

"There were five of us. Three boys and two girls. Like I said, my brothers are both cops. One of my sisters is a doctor. The other is a librarian."

"It sounds like your parents should be proud of their offspring."

"They are."

The waiter interrupted by appearing at their table with the main courses. And they both turned to their meals.

After a bite of his veal shank, he said "This osso bucco is great. Do you want to taste it?"

"If you'll try some of my rack of lamb."

They exchanged some of the food, and she tasted his dish. "It is good."

"So is the lamb."

"It should be. They could feed a family of five for a week on what they're charging."

"Yeah. But you have to crank in the ambiance."

They smiled at each other across the table, and she thought that they were acting like a couple who knew each other pretty well. Joking. Sharing food. The latter was an intimate act, but she told herself not to read too much into it.

Still, she couldn't help feeling that they'd reached another level in the relationship. And she craved more information about him.

"Did you like being a cop?"

"Better than being a P.I."

"Why?"

"I guess I like getting the bad guys off the street. What I do now is more routine."

"Like what?"

"Like snapping pictures of married men and women cheating on their spouses. That's not exactly uplifting."

"I guess not."

"What was your most memorable case—when you were a cop," she asked.

He thought about that for a few minutes. "A hostage situation. A guy I was trailing snatched up a mother and child and threatened to kill them. He knew I was the one on his case. So he insisted that I go in there and exchange myself for the woman and kid."

She sucked in a sharp breath as she pictured the situation. She didn't have any doubts when she said, "You made the exchange."

"Yeah."

"What happened?"

"Well, I had some instructions from my lieutenant. I kept the bad guy talking while the SWAT team got into position."

She swallowed. "That sounds...dangerous."

"Sometimes cops have to deal with danger." His gaze bored into hers. "So—would you...uh...get involved with a man who got into that kind of danger?"

She answered immediately. "Yes."

"You wouldn't resent his profession?"

"It would make every minute with him precious," she said. Then, feeling a little embarrassed, she looked down at her plate.

The conversation had gotten pretty intense. Both of them backed off, each concentrating on the food.

Searching around for another topic, she said, "You were going to tell me what else you were doing this afternoon."

That naughty little boy look flashed across his face again. What had he been up to, exactly?

"What do you mean?" he said guardedly.

"When I asked where else you went besides the mall, you said you'd tell me at dinner."

He sighed. "Okay, I went back to the police department and chatted up one of the officers on the force. According to him, there have been some cases where houses have been broken in to."

"Similar to what happened to me?"

"The difference is that there hasn't been a recent incident where an occupied house was burglarized. See, if the motive is robbery, the perp prefers that nobody's home because it's safer for him."

She nodded.

"Which means either the guy who broke in to your house thought the place was empty, or he was..."

She could see him struggling for a way to say it. "He wanted to...hurt someone," she finished.

"Yeah. Sorry. I don't like giving...bad news."

"It's better to know what we're up against."

"Do we? We still don't know the reason for the attack. The guy could have seen you around the neighborhood and zeroed in on you."

She shivered, and he reached across the table and covered her hand with his.

"What other reason could there be?" she asked.

"We're back to Esther Knight's death." He squeezed her hand and then let it go. "After the police department, I stopped off down the street to speak to those neighbors who wouldn't answer the door when you were in trouble. Mr. Crossman is very sorry he didn't help you out."

"I see."

"He's going to call me if he sees a white van around the neighborhood."

"That's...um...a radical turnabout for him—isn't it?"

"I can be pretty persuasive."

"I know," she answered, her mind going to the activities he'd persuaded her to try. "Actually, you never told me how you got involved in the Esther Knight case," she said quickly.

He waited a beat before saying, "Yeah. Okay. Her family hired me when the police couldn't find any evidence that it was more than a hit and run accident."

"Maybe that's what it was."

"Maybe."

"You don't sound convinced."

"There are some suspicious aspects to her death."

"Like what?"

"Apparently she had gotten a call from a pay phone—and she might have gone out to meet someone. Late at night."

"Why aren't the police following up on that?"

He shifted in his seat. "Sometimes the cops have to set priorities. The phone call could have been a wrong number. They couldn't find any evidence that someone she knew had phoned her. So after a brief investigation, they decided the odds were that it was an accident. They didn't have the time to keep digging. But I do.''

"Yes."

Their eyes met across the table again. "So if I'm wondering whether it's related to the guy who broke in to your house, I'm not trying to scare you. I'm just saying that I want to be cautious when it comes to you."

"Okay. Thanks."

"And I want you to be realistic."

She shivered. "Thanks again."

Under the table, he slid his foot against hers.

"Let's talk about something else," she murmured.

He was leaning back in his chair looking at her in a way that told her their minds had clicked into similar lines again. They had gone from what he called business to the personal without her even realizing they were shifting subjects.

He cleared his throat. "Do you want dessert?"

"I'm not sure I need it. But a cup of cappuccino would be good."

"An excellent idea."

They placed the order, then sipped their coffees.

"Thank you for a really nice evening," she said. "Are you sure I can't pay my share?"

"Absolutely sure," he answered. "I'm glad you liked the restaurant."

"And the company."

"Yes."

They smiled at each other, and she thought again how different he was from the men she usually met.

"What are you thinking?" he asked.

"That I'm glad the Knight family hired you," she blurted, then wished she hadn't put it quite that way.

He laughed. "Murder investigations make strange bedfellows."

She felt a little chill travel over her skin.

He reached across the table and took her hand again. "Sorry. That was a bad choice of words. Cops have a cynical way of viewing the world."

"I'm sure. You've seen a lot more of the sordid side of humanity than most people."

"Yeah." He stroked his fingers over hers. "Which is why it's nice to meet a woman who makes me feel like there's something more to life than the job I do."

"Do I?" she murmured.

"Yes. But I shouldn't hold you captive here much longer. You probably want to get home and get to work."

She felt a surge of disappointment. She hadn't been thinking about work. In fact, she'd had the feeling that the conversation was headed toward a more personal discussion. But he'd just backed away from that. Obviously he wanted to bring the evening to an end.

"Okay," she managed to say.

Zach looked up, located the waiter and signaled for the check, and she stared out the window at the garden lights.

The ride home was a lot like the ride to the Plantation. She'd thought they were getting close. But he'd suddenly acted like he wanted to get rid of her. Well, maybe he had something else he needed to do.

"Thank you for a very nice dinner," she said stiffly, as they entered the living room.

"I enjoyed it," he replied, sounding as awkward as she felt.

She didn't know what else to say now, so she marched back to her bedroom, changed out of the fancy outfit she'd put on for Zach's benefit, then picked up her cell phone to see if there were any messages.

When she went through the sequence of button pushes, she found that Beth had called.

"I haven't heard from you in a couple of days. When I tried to call your home phone, there wasn't any answer. And your voice mail didn't pick up."

Big surprise, Amanda thought as she listened to the message on her cell phone. The answering machine, which was sitting on the floor beside the phone, wasn't connected yet.

"So, how's it going with Zachary Grant?" her friend and editor asked. "In this case, is no news good news? And what's the story with the phone? I'm home this evening. Give me a call if you get back before ten."

Amanda swung her gaze toward the clock on the bedside table. It was before ten, and she felt a pang of guilt. She should certainly have informed Beth about the man who had broken in to her house last night. Last night? It seemed like it was days ago, but it really wasn't.

In the rush of events that had followed their previous conversation, she'd forgotten all about Beth.

Before the end of her dinner conversation with Zach, she would have wanted to talk about him. But dinner had ended on a flat note, and she knew her mood would come across in any discussion with Beth.

With a sigh, Amanda switched off the phone and

put it in its cradle. Another pang of guilt stabbed at her as she looked at the work she'd left on her desk. Really, she was making a career out of her first column. She just had to get the damn thing finished already.

Of course, she had some pretty good excuses now. Someone had broken in to her house. Then Zach had made her move. But she wasn't going to whine to Beth about any of that.

As she stared at the mountain of letters next to her laptop, it seemed like something wasn't quite right. It took several moments for her to figure out that the top letter looked all wrong. She remembered it had been on pink notepaper with a little cat in the corner. Now a piece of notebook paper was sitting on top of it.

A little frisson went through her. Had someone been in here while they were gone and left her a note?

Should she call Zach?

The question made her grimace. What was he going to think—that she couldn't handle a piece of paper by herself?

Quickly she crossed the room and picked it up. The handwriting was bold and masculine. But it was the words on the page that captured her attention. As she looked down at the message, her eyes widened, and she had to reach out with her free hand to steady herself against the edge of the desk.

9

AFTER SCANNING THE LETTER, Amanda forced herself to take a breath, then read more carefully.

Dear Esther,

I'm writing about the woman I've been seeing. We haven't known each other for long, but I like her very much. It's been a long time since a woman has turned me on the way she does. I want to get to know her better, but I worry that she's not going to open up with me. One thing about her is that she thinks she's really au courant about sex. But actually she's kind of prudish. I think it would help her in her work if she let herself go where I'd like to lead her. But I'm hesitant to push her because I don't want to ruin our relationship. If I were going to tell her what I'd like to do, I'd suggest that she let me create a very sensual environment for the two of us. Then I'd like to watch her turn herself on. Well, actually I'd like to tell her the things I'd like her to do. But I get the feeling she'd think that was nasty. So I'm afraid to ask.

Amanda stared down at the letter. He'd like to *what?* Not in this lifetime. Smart of him to be afraid to ask! Although he'd gone ahead and done it anyway. But not to her face. He wasn't man enough for that.

The first thought that leaped into her head was to stomp down the hall and demand to know if he'd lost his mind.

But she'd never been someone who made rash decisions. She looked toward the closed door. She was the one in control now, and she was going to think about what she said before she went off half-cocked.

Half-cocked! That was a great way to put it.

ZACHARY STOOD by the living room window, gazing out into the night. He seemed to have spent a lot of time standing here. Earlier he'd taken a seat on the sofa, but he'd been too nervous to sit still. So he'd gotten up and started pacing the room—and ended up at his favorite spot at the window.

He'd written the letter while he was out, then gone back into the house to leave it with the others. It had seemed like a good idea at the time. But during dinner, he'd started worrying about her reaction. He'd known he couldn't sit there dwelling on it, so he'd rushed her home and sent her to her room, where he knew she was going to discover the piece of notebook paper.

She'd had plenty of time to do that. And she hadn't come back to the living room. So what was going on in there?

Was she going to charge through the door at any minute and ask how dare he make such a raunchy suggestion? Was she going to order him out of the house? What?

He wasn't sure where he'd gotten the guts to write the letter. But he'd known where he'd gotten the idea.

It was while he was walking past the linen shop and seen a gorgeous comforter in the window. It was beige and gold, with a subtle red stripe running through the pattern. And he'd stopped and stared at the beautifully quilted fabric, picturing Amanda lying naked in the middle of the comforter. He'd been immediately hard as a lead pipe.

Impulsively, he'd gone in and bought a queen-size comforter, because he knew that would fit the bed in her room. Then he'd added other details that he knew would enhance the scene. The purchases were in plastic shopping bags locked in the trunk of his car.

He sighed. Maybe he should go outside and take a walk in the dark. Maybe that would cool him off.

Of course, he might find the door bolted when he came back. It would serve him right. He should never have written that letter. Maybe he could tell her he'd been under a kind of compulsion, because it was the truth.

He'd never had such intense desire for a woman. Not even in the early days when he'd been courting his wife. And certainly not since the divorce.

The need for Amanda burned inside him. But he couldn't do what most guys would do with a woman whose essence had crept into their blood. It simply wasn't going to work. So he'd asked for something he could have.

Even now, the thought of what he wanted from her brought a wave of sensual heat sweeping over his body. Yet at the same time, he was suffering the tortures of the damned waiting to find out what she was going to say.

He had been listening for any sound from the bed-

room. The knob turning was like a shotgun shell being pumped into the chamber.

Then her footsteps, light and slow, came down the
hall. He wanted to keep his back to the room, but he
forced himself to turn around and face her. Because
waiting to hear what she was going to say was killing
him—so he might as well get it over with.

The look in her eyes made his breath go shallow.
She didn't speak as they stood regarding each other.
It was agony to keep his arms at his sides and not
fold them defensively across his chest.

Finally she cleared her throat. "Is that why you cut
the dinner-table conversation short?" she asked.

"Yeah," he admitted, glad to get that part out in
the open. "I couldn't sit there any longer wondering
what you were going to do when you found the letter."

"You were right to worry about it. What did you
say—that you thought it would help me in my
work?"

He dragged in a breath and let it out before answering, "That was going too far."

"You're damn right," she shot back, shifting her
weight from one foot to the other. "That's not the
point at all."

"What is the point?" he asked softly.

She didn't answer. But she didn't turn and leave,
either. Just the fact that she was still standing here
gave him back a measure of the hope that he'd abandoned a few moments ago. Maybe she hadn't decided
anything yet. Maybe she was still weighing her decision.

It flashed through his mind that if he closed the
distance between them and took her in his arms, it

might be easier to help her make up her mind. But he wasn't going to try it since it was just as likely that the move was going to blow up in his face.

"You described an activity that a lot of people would find objectionable."

"Do you?"

"Yes."

His hands clenched at his sides. He was thinking he might as well pack up and move out. Or maybe he could sleep out in the car. The comforter was already out there. He could wrap himself up in it. But he stayed where he was, because the idea of leaving her alone when someone meant to do her harm made his stomach knot.

She was speaking again, and her words finally filtered through the buzzing in his brain.

"But then I started thinking... Do I really find it objectionable, or am I just projecting what I learned from my mother? Maybe it was a knee-jerk reaction, so to speak."

He swallowed hard. "Which means what?"

"Which means that I let myself think about it for a while, and...and I..." She stopped, finishing the sentence with a little raise of her shoulder.

"You what?" he pressed, feeling that he was getting back control of the situation.

"The idea made me...aroused."

"Good," he said softly.

"It was exciting, but it was threatening, too."

"Why?"

"Because I'd be putting myself on display."

"Maybe you'd find out something about yourself."

"Maybe," she conceded. "But I think it's more important to find out something about us."

He let that statement hang in the air between them. There were things he could say now, but she wasn't the only one who was nervous. So he fell back on a safe statement. "I've never forced a woman into anything she didn't want to do."

"And have you done this kind of thing before?"

"No. I've been doing things with you that I've never done before. Never wanted to do. But being with you has made me...adventurous."

"Oh."

"I was wandering around the mall, and I started having a fantasy about you. So I went into the bedding shop and bought some things."

"You did?"

"They're in the trunk of my car." Figuring that he might as well take the plunge, he went on rapidly. "What I'd like to do is fix up the bedroom—make it very romantic. Then you can come in, and we'll see what happens."

"Fix up the bedroom?" She gave a nervous little laugh. "What—have you been watching those DYI TV shows where two sets of neighbors spend two days transforming a room in each other's homes?"

"No. I just got a very strong vision of you in a very sensual setting." He couldn't hold back a little grin. "But apparently there are some aspects of DYI that do appeal to me."

It was a relief that she could relax enough to share the joke. With a small laugh, she said, "Apparently."

"So—what do you think? Are you willing to try it?"

"If we agree that I can stop—if this... game...makes me uncomfortable."

"Okay," he said quickly, because it was the only answer he could give her.

"So, why don't you relax and watch television out here. I'll unlock the sliding glass door to your bedroom so I can go in and out without bothering you."

She gave an uncertain little nod. "All right."

"I'll go start getting ready. But first I want to give you something." He left the room, took a deep breath and let it out. He had started on this course, and he didn't seem to be able to stop. Amanda O'Neal had become an obsession, and he didn't like that. But he knew he was reaching for something with her. Something that he wasn't able to put into words—not even in the privacy of his mind.

He stood in the darkened kitchen for a moment—wondering if he was really going ahead with this crazy scheme. Then he reached for the doorknob. Exiting through the kitchen, he opened the car and pulled one of the packages from the trunk.

On the way back in, he locked the door.

When he returned to the living room, he found Amanda sitting on the sofa. She was probably trying to look relaxed, but he could see the tense lines of her body.

He wanted to go to her, take her in his arms, and tell her they were both going to have a great time. But he knew himself. If he embraced her, he was going to start kissing her. And he wasn't going to let go.

And he needed to keep things on track. He'd gotten her agreement. And he wanted very much to go ahead with the little game he'd suggested.

So he stayed where he was, looking from her to the television set. She'd taken his advice. On the screen was one of those DYI shows that he'd seen in passing. *Had* that been where he'd gotten the idea? He saw a man and a woman using steamers and scrapers to peel wallpaper off, inch by inch.

It looked like torture. The show switched to another scene where another couple was arguing with a designer about the deep purple paint he wanted to put on the walls.

"Trust me. You'll love it," the designer said.

Zach laughed. "Sure."

Amanda shifted toward him.

"Interesting choice of TV shows," he commented.

She gave him a long look. "Did you change your mind?

"Of course not!" He stepped toward her and handed over the bag. "I was thinking about what I wanted you to wear, too. And I pictured you in this. Nothing else."

She set the bag on the couch, then reached inside and brought out something thin and silky, wrapped in tissue paper.

He discovered he couldn't draw in a full breath as she carefully unfolded the paper. Inside was a very short dark-blue robe, a silk and lace confection that he knew would look wonderful with her hair and skin.

She didn't speak, and he found he had to break the silence.

"Do you like it?" he asked, hearing the catch in his own voice.

She kept her eyes on the robe, stroking her fingers over the soft fabric. "It's beautiful."

"Then wear it for me when you come into the bedroom."

"And when will that be?" she asked with a small quiver in her voice.

He needed to touch her then—to reassure them both. Crossing the room, he stopped beside the sofa, cupping his hand over her shoulder, feeling the fine structure of her bones beneath his fingers.

He closed his eyes, caressing her. When he heard her little indrawn breath, he roused himself.

"I'll be back as soon I can get ready. In about an hour, I hope." He needed to leave, then. Before he spoiled everything by grabbing her. So he exited the living room and started down the hall. Stepping into the bedroom, he looked around. He already knew the layout. Already knew some of the things he was going to do.

He kept his mind on the tasks at hand, trying not to think about where this was leading. If he thought about that now, he'd be too aroused to get anything done.

So he focused on each small step as he leaned the mattress and the box springs against the wall so that he could get at the bed frame. Quickly he took the frame apart, leaving the wicker headboard in place. Then he opened the sliding glass door and took the frame and the box springs outside. With the substructure of the bed out of the way, he positioned the mattress against the headboard—then went out to get the purchases he'd left in the car.

He smiled as he spread the comforter over the mattress, creating a soft, appealing surface that was low to the floor. Like the bedding in a nomad king's tent. Then he changed the pillowcases for the beige silk ones he'd bought—along with a half dozen other pillows, which he piled against the headboard.

When he was satisfied with the effect, he went on with the other preparations.

AMANDA SAT in the living room, her eyes focused on the television set. Zach had said he'd be about an hour, and she told herself she could still go down the hall and tell him she'd changed her mind. But she knew she wasn't going to disappoint him that way. Or disappoint herself.

So she kept her unseeing gaze on the television screen and played with the fringe of the throw that she'd folded over the back of the sofa. The robe lay on the sofa beside her.

Should she put it on? And sit here feeling half-naked? No, she'd wait until he told her he was ready.

She could hear him in the bedroom, moving things around. What was he doing in there?

Well, she supposed she'd find out soon.

She'd led a pretty tame life. And this was the craziest thing she'd ever agreed to do. And also the most exciting. She could already feel moisture gathering between her legs. Why?

Well, because of what Zach had asked her to do.

She was too keyed up to sit still just waiting for what was to happen. Then an idea struck her. Instead of sitting here with her nerves jumping, she could definitely find something to occupy her time.

Quickly she hurried down the hall, glanced furtively at the closed bedroom door, then slipped into the bathroom, where she opened her makeup kit. Inside was a bottle of red nail polish, which she'd thought she might use while she was down here. She hadn't bothered with it until now.

Grinning, she brought the bottle back to the couch.

After using rolls of tissue to hold her toes apart, she began to polish her toenails.

When she finished, she admired the effect. She was thinking of touching up the little toe on her left foot when she heard the bedroom door open. Then footsteps came slowly down the hall, making a zing of electricity go through her. Quickly, she lowered her legs so her feet were hidden by the coffee table.

Zach walked back into the room, picked up the remote control from the coffee table, and clicked off the set.

When he turned to her, the intensity of his eyes was like a searchlight. She might have ducked away; instead she raised her head questioningly toward him—struggling to keep herself steady without taking her lower lip between her teeth.

"It's time to put on that robe," he said, and she knew from the little break in his voice that he wasn't as calm and collected as he looked.

She stood, stiffening her legs when she felt herself start to sway. Reaching down, she gathered up the robe.

"I'll put it on. But you have to do something for me, too."

"What?"

"Take off your shirt. If we're going to do this, I need to see your naked chest."

"I can do better than that," he growled.

"How?"

"You'll have to wait and see, won't you?"

She looked away from the gleam in his eyes, once again questioning her sanity. Her mouth was dry as she snatched up the robe and headed for the bathroom.

ZACH STOOD THERE with his pulse pounding in his ears as he watched Amanda disappear into the bathroom. She was really going to do it. At least he hoped to hell she wasn't going to chicken out now.

The sound of the lock clicking released him. Shaking his head to clear away the fog, he headed for his own room.

He never wore pajamas. But he'd spent some time considering how he should be dressed for this evening's activities. Seeing a display of very sexy-looking men's nightwear had helped him make up his mind.

He'd picked out a burgundy pair of pajamas with a subtle pattern of navy stripes.

Closing the door to his room, he began to pull off his clothing. First his shoes. Then his shirt. Finally his slacks and shorts. The last part was a little difficult to manage because he was so turned on that his huge swollen erection was definitely in the way.

But he'd never heard of a guy who couldn't have sex because he was trapped in his clothing. So he eased the pants off. Then pulled on the pajama bottoms. The pants had no button or zippered fly. Only a folded-over slit in the front, and he had to maneuver himself so that he wasn't poking through the fabric.

He stopped and leaned his head and shoulders against the door, feeling the blood pounding in his veins. Particularly in the lower part of his body.

He thought about what she'd see when they met again. His arms were good—nicely muscled. And his shoulders were broad. Did Amanda like a guy with hair on his chest? Some women didn't. He hoped she didn't mind a nice dark thicket.

Well, it was too late to think about that now. He wasn't going to shave it.

When he heard the lock on the bathroom door click again, he closed his eyes for a moment, then stepped into the hall.

The light was dim, but the sight of Amanda in that robe took his breath away. She'd brushed out her hair so that it was a golden halo around her head. She'd put on a little makeup. Not much, just a little eye shadow and blusher that subtly brought out the natural beauty of her features.

He looked down the length of her body, pausing to admire the tight points of her nipples and the golden triangle of hair he could just make out at the top of her legs.

Her feet were bare, and he felt something inside his chest turn over when he saw the red polish on her nails. She hadn't been wearing the polish yesterday, because he would have noticed. So he knew she'd done that for him. For his pleasure, and he had to press his hands against his thighs to keep from reaching for her.

When he glanced up, he saw she was looking at him with frank appreciation. Maybe chest hair turned her on.

But it wasn't his upper body that she mentioned.

"Nice pajamas," she said, and he knew she could clearly see the erection poking out the fabric.

"I'm glad you like them," he managed to say. Then, "Come see if you like the bedroom."

He stepped aside to let her pass, then caught his breath as one of her silk-clad arms brushed against his.

Again, he had to clamp down on the impulse to

reach for her. He wanted to drag her body against his. He wanted to feel the length of her pressed against his heated flesh. But he knew that was the wrong thing to do. He had spent a lot of time setting up his fantasy, and they both needed to see it through. At least, he did. He hoped she could stay with him.

She stepped forward, into the bedroom.

He couldn't see her face, and when he heard her make a small sound, he found he was fighting to breathe around the lump that suddenly clogged his throat as he waited for her reaction to his evening's work.

10

AMANDA HADN'T BEEN SURE what she was going to find. She took several steps into the room and stopped short, feeling dazed as she looked around. The last time she'd been in the bedroom, it had been full of typical beach-house decor. Now it was totally transformed—into a romantic and mysterious environment.

Wanting to see more, she glided forward, curious about how Zach had worked the transformation.

Apparently, he'd carefully considered each detail. The bed was now low to the floor, a soft platform covered by a beautiful gold and beige comforter.

He'd moved the dresser to the end of the bed, closing in the space. Then he'd piled two inviting mounds of pillows on the bed. One was at the headboard. The other was at the foot, with the back of the dresser serving as another backrest.

The effect was to create a sumptuous, private cave for two people. And the effect was enhanced by gauzy bed draperies made of mosquito netting that he'd cleverly hung from the ceiling fan.

They came down in a swirl of translucent fabric, on either side of the headboard, enclosing it like an old-fashioned bed canopy—but more open and airy.

A scarf-covered lamp in one corner provided romantic illumination—as did the candles he'd set on the dresser and on top of the armoire.

No man had ever gone to this kind of trouble to set a romantic scene for her, and she was awed and a little intimidated—if she was truthful.

"It's beautiful," she murmured, without turning to look at him. When she heard the breath ease out of him, she knew he'd been waiting for her approval.

"It's for you—for us."

"Are you sure you don't watch those DYI shows?" she asked, because her nerves were begging her to keep the conversation going.

"I've seen a little. But mostly this is from my imagination. For how I wanted to see you."

He didn't touch her, but she was so aware of him standing behind her that she felt her skin tingling.

"Where did you get all the pillows?"

"Some are extras I found in the closets. I bought some." He laughed, "And I stuffed some pillowcases with extra bedding. But let's not spoil the illusion by going into details."

"Okay."

He stepped up behind her, curving his hands around her shoulders, his fingers pressing into her skin, suffusing heat through her body like a sudden firestorm.

"I know why you're asking so many questions. Don't be nervous."

"I'm not…nervous," she lied.

He bent to stroke his lips against her cheek. "Good, because if you keep me waiting much longer, you're going to be responsible for my having a heart attack," he growled.

She gave a half glance over her shoulder and saw

the rigid lines of his face. He knew she could still back out, but she wasn't going to disappoint either one of them. Licking suddenly dry lips, she knelt, keeping her knees pressed together as she eased herself onto the mattress.

He let out another pent-up breath. "Sit up at the headboard end. Fix the pillows so you're comfortable."

Feeling strangely light-headed, she did as he asked. Yet she still had trouble imagining herself going through with what he had described. In the back of her mind, she was thinking that she could change the rules as they went along. In fact, she knew she had to change the rules if this was going to work for her.

But she wasn't going to tell him that. Not yet.

To keep from letting him see her doubts, she turned and fussed with the pillows, making herself a comfortable place to relax, although she knew that relaxation was impossible.

As she settled into the plush backrest, she felt charged with a growing arousal. Did it show on her face? On her body? She kept herself from looking down at the tight, hard points of her nipples that must be visible through the silky robe.

Zachary Grant could arouse her without even touching her. But then she already knew that.

Trying to distract herself, she glanced at the white netting on either side of her. It made a gauzy tent around her head and shoulders, helping her feel enfolded in a private world.

Well, not exactly private, she thought with a sudden zing of awareness as she felt the mattress shift. When she looked up, she saw that Zach had walked around the other side of the bed and joined her on the

mattress, settling into the other mound of pillows—
the ones that he'd arranged against the back of the
dresser.

She could see then that he'd made the bed surface
longer by padding the end of the mattress with additional bedding to extend the area a few feet. But
still, when she'd imagined this scene, she hadn't expected him to be that close to her.

She'd been picturing him sitting on the other side
of the room. Now he was right here in bed with her,
and she could easily reach out and grab one of his
bare feet.

Which was what *he* did. Sliding his hand several
inches across the comforter, he took her right foot in
his hand, stroking his thumb along the instep, sending
little prickles of electricity up her leg.

"I like that nail polish," he said. "It looks sexy.
Did you do that for me?"

"Yes—and to distract myself while I was waiting
for you to finish in here."

She closed her eyes and pressed her palms against
the comforter, focusing on the touch of his hand as
he continued to stroke her foot.

"Are you okay?" he asked.

"I think so."

"You are so beautiful. I love the way that robe
looks on you, and I love the contrast with the pillows
and the comforter."

"Why do you want to do this?" she asked. "I
mean this whole thing."

"It's very stimulating," he answered immediately.
"Don't you agree?"

"You know it is. But there's no reason you have

to stay at the other end of the bed. You could come up here and lie down with me.

"I could. But then I wouldn't get to play out my fantasy."

"Maybe I can't play it out."

"Oh, I think you can." His gaze dropped to the front of her robe, where the tight beads of her nipples pointed toward him. "I know you're already aroused—just by this much. And we've barely gotten started."

She couldn't deny it.

"Do you think this is wicked?"

Her throat was suddenly dry, but she managed to answer, "No."

"Good. So let's see how far we can take this."

His words made her pulse suddenly pound. What was he going to want from her?

All he said was, "Why don't you open the top two buttons of that robe. Just so I can see the creamy skin below your neck."

She could do that, she thought, as she lifted her hands from the mattress, then struggled to keep her fingers from trembling as she fumbled with the buttons.

He stared at that triangle of exposed skin. "Nice. Very nice."

How could something so simple make her so hot, she wondered.

His next words came to her over the buzzing in her brain as he said, "Lift your hands for me. Let me see you cup your breasts."

The only way she could do what he asked was to close her eyes first. Behind her closed lids, she felt as though she were in a dream world. With deliberate slowness, she moved her hands from the buttons of the robe and cupped her breasts, feeling a stab of arousal.

It helped when she heard him draw in a quick breath so that she knew he was reacting to this fantasy scene as strongly as she was herself.

His voice was thick as he said, "Brush your fingers over the nipples. Stroke the edges. Do what feels good to you."

She did it, her own touch burning her body.

"Is that good?" he asked, his voice close to her and yet far away.

"Yes..." she managed to say, because speech was almost beyond her.

"Do you like the silky feel of the robe between your hands and your breasts?"

She gave a small nod.

"But I'll bet it would feel even better without that layer of fabric. So unbutton some more of that robe for me. Just the top part if you want."

She kept her eyes closed as she fumbled with the buttons, opening the next two.

"One more," he growled. "You need to unbutton one more."

She did as he asked, waiting for what must come next. Was he going to ask her to take off the robe?

"That's a very tantalizing picture," he murmured. "But I'll like it even more if you push the fabric to the sides. All the way to the sides so I can see your breasts."

Her fingers were trembling as she did his bidding, feeling the cool air of the room on her hot skin.

"That's so beautiful," he murmured. "I knew you

would be. But not this stunning. Seeing this view of you is breathtaking.''

She could hear the raspy sound of her own breathing. And his.

"Touch them again. Show me the things you like. Make yourself hot for me.''

She took her lower lip between her teeth as she found her breasts again with her hands.

"Tug on the nipples. Twist them a little, if that feels good. Run your fingernails over the tips.''

All of that felt good, and she couldn't hold back a small gasp.

"You need to come, don't you?''

She could only answer with a little whimpering sound.

"Good. That's good. Unbutton the rest of the robe for me.''

Her fingers felt thick and clumsy as she did what he asked.

"Now spread the fabric apart all the way. Let me see you.''

As she did, she heard him draw in a quick, sharp breath. "Lord, that's so beautiful.''

She felt exposed and so hot that she wondered why she didn't set the mattress on fire.

His voice caressed her, asking for more. "Open your legs a little. Let me see that part of you. The hidden, female part.''

She felt as though he were the one in control of her body as she shifted her legs.

"That's so sexy. You're so turned on, aren't you? So wet and swollen. You need to do something about that, don't you? So touch yourself there.''

Her fingers obeyed him, taking a gliding stroke through her own hot, distended tissue.

Her hips rocked against her hand, increasing the pleasure of her own touch. She wanted to come now. Needed to come.

But not yet. Not quite yet.

She dragged in a steadying breath, opened her eyes and looked straight into the heat and intensity of his gaze.

His pupils were dilated. His whole body was rigid as he focused on her.

"I can't do this by myself," she said. "I need you with me."

"I am with you."

"I need to know this is turning you on as much as it's turning me on."

"It is. You know damn well it is."

"Then show me. Open the fly of your pajamas. Let me see your cock," she said, focusing on keeping her voice from quivering.

"I…"

"You have to play, too," she said, wondering what she would do if he refused, because her body was so supercharged now that she felt like she was going to explode.

For several racing heartbeats, she wondered if he was going to do what she asked. Then he reached down and opened the pants, bringing his erection out of the fabric. He was red and swollen, and there was a drop of semen at the tip. She smiled as she thought that she had done this to him.

The head of his erection was pointed toward her, and when he let his hand drop away, it gave a small jerk.

She summoned the strength to say, "No."

"No what?" he asked, his voice low and strained.

"Let me see you touch yourself. Let me see what makes *you* hot."

She could see he didn't want to do it. Well, too bad. She had said she wasn't going to play this game by herself.

"Run your finger around the glans," she said, then felt a thrill of triumph when he did it.

"Does that feel good?" she asked.

He didn't speak, but she knew by the look on his face that it did.

"Your turn," he growled. "Dip your fingers into your vagina, then drag them up to your clit."

She knew it wouldn't take much to make her self-destruct now. His words were almost enough to do it.

But she hung on to her resolve. "You, too," she demanded. "You stroke yourself, too. The way you do it when you make yourself come."

He froze, and she thought for a moment that he was going to call a halt to the fantasy. Then his hand began to move. And hers did, too. She kept her gaze on him as she felt herself rushing toward climax, stroking with her fingers, rocking her hips, listening to the sound of his breath rushing in and out of his lungs, watching his hand moving, hard and fast.

Her own need built as she touched herself and watched him doing the same. She couldn't hold back any longer. Orgasm rocketed through her, just as she heard him gasp and saw his cock pumping as creamy liquid squirted from the tip.

She collapsed back against the cushions, breathing hard, watching the look of satisfaction—and surprise—that spread across his face.

Maybe he hadn't expected to be this involved. But she'd made sure she wasn't the only one participating intimately in the fantasy he'd set up.

Wordlessly, she held out her arms to him, and he came up to her end of the bed, gathering her to him.

"Thank you," he murmured. "That was mind-blowing."

"Yes."

She waited for him to say more. She wanted to know how he felt about what they had just done. But she suspected he wasn't going to tell her. Not yet.

Guys weren't great at articulating their feelings. In some ways, what they'd done together was more intimate than if they'd had intercourse. And she wanted to tell him that—and have him share his feelings. But she suspected that if she tried to get into a conversation, he'd accuse her of spoiling the experience.

And perhaps he'd be right. What they'd just done existed in a place out of time. In another universe. He was still there with her, actually. And for now she would be content to have him hold her.

For a few moments, he did hold her, nuzzling his mouth against her neck and hair, stroking her damp skin under the robe that she still wore.

She was thinking that maybe they'd both be more comfortable if they got undressed. But she forgot what she was going to say when the stroking fingers moved to her breasts and down to the juncture of her legs. His touch was light, almost teasing. But she found her arousal building once again.

"Zach?"

"I want to taste you. All of you," he growled. Leaning over, he nibbled at her collarbone, then swept the hollow of her throat with his tongue.

"Let me," he murmured, and he began to nibble and lick his way down her body.

She lay back and closed her eyes, his mouth sending a tide of heat sweeping through her.

He was good at this, good at all the skills of pleasing a woman.

He played with her abdomen, then combed his fingers through the curly triangle of hair just below.

"I wanted to do that. I ached to touch you."

"And I ached for you to do it," she told him.

He didn't answer, only lowered his head, finding her throbbing sex with his mouth, making her moan with the pleasure of his skilled caress.

He brought her to another mind-blowing climax, using his tongue and his lips, two of his fingers sliding in and out of her as he worked her clit with his mouth.

And she was helpless to do anything besides dig her fingers into his hair and let him have his way with her.

AFTERWARDS, she knit her fingers with his, holding him beside her because she suspected he might be getting ready to leave the bed.

"Stay with me."

"I should let you rest."

"I want you to sleep here. Please don't leave."

Long seconds passed while she waited for his answer. "You're not afraid I'm going to wake up and try to attack you?"

"Not at all."

He waited a moment, and she held her breath, knowing he might still leave.

Finally he said, "Okay. But I should blow out the candles. And turn off the light."

She let out the breath she'd been holding. As she watched him move about the room, dousing the flames, her gaze dropped to the front of his pajamas. He was as hard as he'd been when they'd sat across from each other on the bed, but she had the feeling he wasn't going to let her do anything about it.

"Let me get the covers and get rid of some of these pillows."

She watched him remove the pile of pillows from the far end of the bed, then open the closet and come back with a sheet and blanket, which he spread over the bed, before climbing underneath with her.

His total focus was on the domestic tasks, as though he were distancing himself from her.

In the darkness she asked, "Can I do anything for you?"

"I'm fine," he said in a tight voice that told her he didn't want to say any more.

She had learned enough about him so that she didn't press the point. But as she moved some of the pillows to the floor beside the bed, she was thinking that he had done this before. Kept her from giving him the release that most guys would demand. In fact, the only times he'd climaxed had been…when she wasn't touching him.

There was always a period when a man couldn't get an erection after having an orgasm. But Zach was clearly aroused. So that wasn't the problem.

So what was going on here?

She wanted to turn the light back on and demand that they have a discussion about why he was denying himself additional sexual satisfaction. But she knew this wasn't the right time to talk about it. So she pretended she was perfectly content to let things stand as she snuggled down beside him.

11

AMANDA WOKE EARLY, feeling wonderfully refreshed and rested. A smile flickered on her lips when she remembered going to sleep in Zach's arms. But when she turned to the far side of the bed, she found that Zach wasn't there.

A stab of disappointment pierced her. She'd wanted to wake up next to him, she'd wanted that very much. But he'd chosen to leave.

Getting up, she pulled off the robe she was still wearing, then found some shorts and a T-shirt in the dresser that was still pushed against the bed.

Then she gazed around the room. It had looked sensual and romantic the evening before. The magic Zach had created still clung to it in the morning light. Maybe because she wanted it to.

Should she ask him to change it back? She wasn't sure what she wanted yet.

After a stop in the bathroom, she poked her head in Zach's room and was relieved to find his clothing still hanging in the closet. She'd been half afraid that he would clear out before they could talk. But he was still here. Somewhere.

He wasn't in the living room or the kitchen, but he'd made a pot of coffee.

She decided to pour herself a cup, then changed her mind and hurried back down the hall where she stripped off her clothing again and took a quick shower.

He still wasn't home by the time she'd partially dried her hair and gotten dressed again. She was pacing barefoot back and forth across the length of the living room when she saw a flicker of movement through the window.

Looking outside, she saw Zach and breathed out a little sigh.

He was speeding up the long driveway, dressed in shorts, running shoes, and a T-shirt that clung damply to his broad shoulders.

He opened the door quietly, then stopped short when he saw her standing in the living room.

"Hi," she said.

"Hi."

"You were up early."

"So were you."

"I often go for an early run," he answered stiffly.

The tone of his voice challenged her to make something of it, and she knew suddenly that she wasn't going to. Last night, as she had lain beside him, she'd sensed that it wasn't the right time to ask questions. As far as she could see, nothing had changed.

"I was thinking we should get some groceries," she said. "There's nothing in the house to eat, and I'd like to fix some breakfast."

The mundane suggestion seemed to relax him. "Let me take a shower, and I'll be ready to go. You can write me a list."

She nodded, thinking of the phrase her mother used to use. *Sending a man to do a woman's job.* She'd said that there were some things men simply weren't cut out to do. And grocery shopping was one of those things. But she wasn't going to argue with Zach until after his shower.

Fortified with a cup of his strong coffee laced with a nice shot of cream and caramel, she was waiting for him when he came back.

After pouring himself some of the coffee and taking a sip, he asked, "Where's the list?"

"I didn't write it." She folded her arms across her chest. "I'm going to the store with you."

He studied her defiant posture. "Not a good idea. You do remember that a man broke in to your house and attacked you? You do remember that's why we moved to a different location? So he couldn't find you."

She ignored the pointed reminders of why they were hiding out. Instead she said, "You took me out to dinner."

"That was different. An out-of-the-way, upscale restaurant. A grocery store is right in the thick of things. The guy who attacked you could be hanging around public places, hoping you'll show up."

"So we go to one that's on the other side of town instead of the one in the shopping center down the road," she argued. "You can deck me out with a disguise so the...the assailant won't even know who I am."

"A list would be better," he insisted.

"I'm not good at making lists. I want to see what's there. If the tomatoes look good, I want some. How are you at evaluating fresh produce?"

"Not great," he admitted with the look of a man who had somehow backed himself into a corner.

With victory in sight, she pressed, "This will only take an hour. Then I promise to stay in this nice cozy little hideout—with no contacts besides you and the ducks out there.''

He sighed. ''Okay. We get in and out of the store quickly. Do you have a hat you can pull down over your face.''

''I've got a sun hat.''

He thought for a moment. ''You usually wear shorts and a T-shirt, so wear something different—like a sun dress. Tuck your hair up under the hat. And wear more makeup than usual—so your face is different.''

She nodded and hurried back to her room to follow directions. Her wardrobe was limited, but she pulled on a simple knit dress and topped it with a camp shirt; she dug her straw sun hat out of the closet. Then she slathered on some makeup and made her lips twice their normal size. She completed the outfit with a pair of sandals that matched her hat.

When she returned to the living room, Zach was wearing an outfit she hadn't seen—worn jeans, a jeans jacket, cowboy boots, and a hat.

She did a double take, then grinned. ''Are you going for the country and western look?''

''Something like that,'' he answered as he studied her choice of clothing. ''Do you have sunglasses?''

''Yes.''

''Wear them, and keep them on in the store.'' He shifted from one foot to the other. ''Let's get this over with. The sooner you're tucked back home, the better I'll like it.''

''You can go on record as opposing the expedition.''

''Yeah. Right.'' He led her outside, then hesitated.

"What are you waiting for?" she asked, hoping she hadn't made him change his mind.

"I'm thinking about which vehicle to take. I don't like either choice, but I guess mine is better, since yours was parked at the old house the whole time you were there."

St. Stephens was a small town, Tony thought. If O'Neal and her boyfriend were still here, he had a decent chance of running into them. So he'd hung around, hoping for a break.

He'd cruised the shopping center parking lots and the discount mall, but so far he hadn't seen either O'Neal's little Toyota or the guy's Honda, and he was wondering if they had access to another vehicle.

He'd done that himself. He'd found an isolated house where newspapers were piling up next to the mailbox.

So he'd come back that night, let himself in and found an itinerary from a travel agency telling him that the couple who lived there wouldn't be back from Italy for a week. After parking the van in the woods nearby, he borrowed their old Mustang. The guy probably kept it around because it was a classic model. Tony liked it because it didn't have a modern ignition or alarm system.

He was planning to put it back in a couple of days, well before the owners returned home. But for now it was the perfect option.

As he pulled into the parking lot outside the Acme, he was thinking he was getting low on groceries. So he might as well kill two birds with one stone and go in to pick up some food. Easy stuff that he could eat while he was driving around looking for Dr. O'Neal and Mr. Buttinski.

AMANDA WATCHED ZACH as he did a slow tour of the shopping center parking lot. When he stopped beside a white van, she felt a little shiver go over her skin. "Is that him?" she whispered.

"No. This van's got a ladder rack on the top."

"Oh," she answered, thinking that was the kind of detail she wouldn't have spotted in a million years, since vehicles were just a means of transportation, as far as she was concerned.

There were other vans in the lot, but none of them was white. So Zach pulled into a space near the entrance to the grocery store, then turned to her.

"We're going to play a very friendly couple. I'll have my arm around you. And you can say cute little twitty things that are completely out of character."

She gaped at him. "Is that necessary?"

"Yeah. Because it's not something you'd do in public."

"How do you know?"

"I know," he answered with confidence as he opened his door and climbed out.

She had no choice but to follow suit. He came around to her side of the car and took her arm, holding her against his side as he pressed the remote control lock. And he kept her beside him as they made their way into the grocery.

"Don't make us too conspicuous," she murmured as they took a cart.

"I won't," he answered, loosening his hold on her waist but not letting go. She slid him a sideways glance, seeing the proprietary look on his face.

They'd both felt awkward when he'd come in this morning. She'd guessed that he'd gone running in the first place as a way of avoiding her. Now they were out in public, and he was using the opportunity to get close to her again. They could have been playing a couple who were angry at each other. But he'd chosen to do just the opposite.

Because he wanted to get close! But he didn't know how to get past the awkward morning-after.

For just a moment, she laid her head on his shoulder, and he looked down at her.

"We'll get in and out of here fast," he said, completely misunderstanding her reaction.

"I have every confidence in you," she answered sweetly.

She liked the solid feel of his body next to hers. She'd like the solid feel of it *on top* of hers, she suddenly thought.

"What?"

"I was just looking at those nice ripe peaches," she said. "See, if you hadn't brought me along, I would never have known they were here. How would you like some peach cobbler?"

"Sounds good. But peach pie would be even better."

She laughed. "Peach pie is too much trouble. I'm not going to make a pie crust, even for you."

"You could get one of those premade frozen ones."

"Hmm. Okay."

She picked out a dozen peaches, then looked at the salad makings. "Do you mind those salads in a bag?"

He stroked his hand over her shoulder. "Any kind of home-cooked meal would be fantastic."

"Then let's get some onions and some green peppers."

"For what?"

"A surprise."

They were looking at each other, grinning, and she knew she shouldn't be enjoying this so much. It was like playing house with Zachary Grant, and getting too attached to the idea would be a mistake, because in a few days he'd have to go back to New Jersey, and she'd still be down here working on her column and her book. But really, she could do that anywhere. She didn't have to stay in St. Stephens.

His voice brought her out of her reverie. "What are you thinking?"

What was she thinking? Was she fantasizing about moving in with him? She gave the shopping cart a quick shove, heading for the dairy department. "Nothing."

TONY SPOTTED THEM almost as soon as he walked into the store. They probably thought they were in disguise. But he'd studied Amanda O'Neal too carefully to miss her—even with that sun hat and all that makeup. He'd know her anywhere because his total focus had been on her for the past week.

He'd been afraid that he'd lost her. Now he felt a surge of elation as he ducked back into an aisle of canned fruit and vegetables.

He peered out, but O'Neal and Buttinski were so wound up with each other that he knew it would take a stack of cereal boxes falling on them to break their concentration.

The guy was decked out as a cowboy. At least he

assumed it was the same guy, although he couldn't be absolutely sure.

Tony hadn't thought that O'Neal had a boyfriend, but the two of them sure looked cozy. Well, they'd better enjoy it while it lasted, because he was going to break them up—permanently.

He kept a good way behind them, putting a few things in his cart as they stopped in the dairy department. Next they headed toward the meat section and, after choosing a few cuts of beef, continued shopping throughout the rest of the store for about thirty minutes.

Tony waited while they paid for their purchases, then abandoned his own cart so he could follow them into the parking lot.

They walked toward the Honda he'd seen the other day. The guy had screwed him up then, but it wasn't going to happen again, Tony thought as he watched them stow their groceries in the trunk of the car, then pull out of the parking lot.

He kept well back as they swung onto the highway. When he saw them make a turn onto a side road, he followed.

It was a little hard to see where they were going because he had to be really careful not to get spotted. But finally he saw the car turn into a long drive leading to a house he could barely see through the trees.

Hot damn! He was back in business.

AMANDA HAD HOPED the feeling of closeness would last when they got home. But as soon as they were back in the house, she sensed that Zach was on edge.

He helped her put away the groceries, then stood looking at her uncertainly.

"I'll go put the bedroom back the way it was," he said, and she knew that he had only brought up the subject out of necessity.

"I kind of like it the way it is," she managed to say.

"Okay."

"I promised to make breakfast if we went shopping," she offered.

"You don't have to bother. I can just grab something. I have to write up a report on what's been happening with the case."

A report, she thought. Probably it wasn't going to include last night's activities.

"There's no need for you to eat in your room. I was thinking about making an omelette. Eggs. Ham. Green pepper. Onion. Cheese. Tomatoes. Are you sure I can't persuade you to wait on your report?"

She watched him weighing his options. A dry report versus a mouthwatering breakfast.

"That sounds delicious," he finally answered. "A lot better than a fast-food breakfast."

"How are you at chopping onions?"

"So that's why you wanted me to stick around!" She laughed. "Partly."

As they fixed what was now brunch, she worked to keep the easy mood going between them. She was enjoying his company and didn't want him to disappear into his room.

He watched her cooking the onions, peppers and ham in a large skillet. As she poured in all the eggs, he stared into the pan.

"Wait a minute. Who gets that big omelette?" he asked.

"Both of us. I read in a book that you can make one big one and divide it in portions."

"If it works, I'll bow to your expertise."

My expertise as Esther Scott? she wanted to ask, but she kept that question to herself.

She wanted to talk about last night. She wanted to know what was going on with Zach. But she understood she was going to have to find the right time and the right place.

So she kept the easy camaraderie going during the meal, accepted his help cleaning up the kitchen and let him go off to work up his notes—if that was what he was really doing.

She'd been using the desk in the bedroom, but she knew the new arrangement would be distracting. So she found her computer and the letters that Zach had set on the closet floor and carried them to the living room.

The good thing about a laptop was that you could work anywhere, she mused as she settled down on the sofa, with the computer on her lap and the letters in a pile beside her.

Today she was determined to get enough material for the column. So, although she hated herself for doing it, she started looking for questions that were easy to answer.

Dear Esther,
I'm sixteen years old and I haven't gotten my period yet. Is there something wrong with me?
                              Sixteen in Atlanta.

That was easy enough to deal with.

Dear Sixteen,
You might want to make an appointment for a physical exam. But likely there is nothing wrong with you. Girls get their periods at different ages. You could be just a late-bloomer.

She looked at her answer, then realized that there might be a problem. She hadn't read any letters in Esther's previous columns from anyone in her midteens. Was there some age limit on who could get answers from the column?

She could simply skip the letter, she knew. But it suddenly made her remember that Beth had called the day before, and she hadn't answered. So she got her cell phone from the charger in the kitchen and dialed her editor.

The receptionist put her right through.

"Amanda, thank God," her friend said as soon as she got on the line. "I tried ringing you again this morning, and the phone at your place is disconnected. What's going on?"

"Two nights ago, someone broke in to my house."

"Good grief! Are you all right?"

"Yes. I called Zach, and he chased the guy off. But he thinks the incident could be connected with Esther's death."

She heard Beth suck in a sharp breath.

"Well, he got the real estate company to let me move. That's why you couldn't get me on the phone."

"Very resourceful. Is he there with you?" Beth asked.

"Yes. He wanted to stay around and make sure nothing else happens."

"Good. He seemed like he knew his job. I feel much better knowing you're with him."

"Yes," Amanda agreed, wondering what else to say.

"How is it going with the two of you?"

Amanda hesitated.

"He's there, so you can't say much?" Beth guessed.

"In the house, yes."

"Then just answer yes or no. Do you like him?"

"Yes."

"And he obviously likes you, or he wouldn't still be there."

"Well…"

"Is he a good lover?" Beth asked suddenly.

"Yes," Amanda answered. Everything she'd done with him had been good, although she wouldn't call it making love—not in the strictest sense of the word.

"I called to ask you about the column," she said, changing the subject. "Am I allowed to answer questions from teenagers?"

"What kind of questions?"

"There's one from a sixteen-year-old who's worried that she hasn't gotten her period yet."

"That's a little young for our audience."

"Yeah, I was afraid of that."

"How's the column going?"

"With everything that's been happening, I haven't had much chance to work on it. But I'm back on track now."

"Good. Why don't you e-mail me what you've got in the next few days."

Amanda swallowed. "Sure."

"Hang on to Zach. He's a keeper."

"Beth!"

"Okay, you're the one writing the advice column."

"Yes, and I need to get back to work," Amanda said quickly. After giving Beth her new number, she hung up.

The phone started to buzz, and she realized that she'd clamped her hand around it and pushed some button or other. Quickly, she hung up, then looked toward the hall to see if Zach was going to come investigate the noise. When his door didn't open, she breathed out a small sigh.

Then she looked down at the letter she'd answered, folded it up again and erased her response.

She'd been trying for something easy, and all she'd done was waste a bunch of time.

Well, she'd better find something more suitable and write out a reply—in the next hour.

12

HER LIPS SET IN A GRIM LINE, Amanda opened another letter. It was from a woman whose new husband was going out with the boys every night.

She could answer that one, but it sounded more like a question for Dear Abby.

The next letter was more promising.

Dear Esther,

My husband and I have been married for a year, and I think we have a very good sexual relationship, except for one complaint that I hear from time to time.

He's always the one who asks for sex. He's the one who decides what we're going to do. We always have a good time together in the bedroom. But he says he'd like for me to initiate some of the things we do. Maybe I'm shy. Maybe I'm old-fashioned. Maybe I'm afraid that he won't like my ideas. But I'm more comfortable letting him make the first move. Can you give me any suggestions for how to change this situation?

Old-fashioned Wife

Amanda read the letter again. Well, she'd finally found a problem that was easy to address, and one that troubled a lot of women. She began to type her reply.

Dear Old-fashioned,
Don't be shy about telling your husband what you want. He's obviously eager for you to show him how much you want him by making the first move. And don't be afraid that he'll think less of you for initiating a sexual encounter. More likely, he'll be thrilled if you tell him what you'd like to do together.

Amanda sat back and read through her answer. It was good enough, she supposed. But she had the feeling there was more she could say.

While she was in the middle of trying to fix up her answer, her hands stopped moving on the computer keys.

She was trying to make this woman feel comfortable with initiating sexual encounters. Maybe she should be taking her own advice.

Zach had wondered aloud whether she had enough sexual experience to write an advice column. She'd assured him that she did, although privately she'd admitted that there were a lot of things she hadn't done. Of course, that list was a bit shorter since she'd met him. She'd gained some memorable experience, but everything they had done together had been his idea.

His wanting to do those things with her was arousing, she admitted, since she was trying to be totally honest with herself. She couldn't think about any of their encounters without getting turned on.

And last night he'd gone to considerable effort to

set up a scene that obviously fulfilled one of his very erotic fantasies.

She'd gone along with him, because she wanted to connect with him on an intimate level. More than that, although she'd been hesitant at first, she'd had the courage to admit that she found the idea he'd described exciting.

Still, none of the things they'd done together had come from her own imagination. Maybe because she was too down-to-earth to have more than the most basic fantasies. She'd never thought about setting up a room like a love cave. Or thinking about what she was going to wear in that very erotic setting.

Perhaps it was time for her to be a little bolder in their relationship.

Of course, there was danger in going that route. What if her fantasies totally turned him off?

Well, better to find out now than later.

She knew a look of determination was plastered on her face as she shoved the letters back into the canvas sack where they'd come from, then saved her file and turned off her computer.

"Lighten up," she murmured to herself. "This is supposed to be fun."

Right. Fun. Still, her mouth turned dry as she walked down the hall and glanced at the closed door to Zach's room. She might have paused there, but she knew he was probably listening to her footsteps. So she sailed on past and entered her own room, where she quietly closed the door behind her and switched on the overhead light.

Ignoring her own jumping nerves, she went over to the bed. First she folded up the sheet and blanket that he'd covered them with the night before. Then she shook out his beautiful comforter and straightened it on the bed.

Next she tackled the mound of pillows, fluffing some up and moving others to the side and out of the way, so that the bed was still opulent looking but better designed for more conventional lovemaking. Which was what she had in mind this time around.

She didn't allow herself to think about what it would mean if Zach refused to have intercourse with her. She simply went about trying to make it happen.

Her throat tightened. Was she setting herself up for disappointment? She was betting that wasn't going to be true.

She liked the room Zach had created, and she left most of his romantic touches intact. Like the lamp with the scarf over it.

First she closed the blinds. Then she turned on the lamp and switched off the overhead light, pleased with the romantic effect it created.

But not yet. When she got Zach in here, she didn't want him to know she was setting anything up. So she switched on the overhead light again to finish her preparations.

With a rising sense of excitement, she thought about what she was going to wear. The robe he'd bought her was one possibility. But she wanted to put her own stamp on the encounter, so she thought about what clothing she'd brought with her. Not a lot to work with, unfortunately. But she did have a few things that might work.

Shucking off her dress, she began opening drawers, looking for the white camisole top she'd bought in one of the shops along Main Street.

It was thin cotton, with ribbons running through the

straps and lace at the top and bottom edge, and she'd planned to wear it under a sweater.

Now she pulled off her shirt and bra and tried it on alone.

By itself, it looked both demure and very provocative. She could see her nipples clearly through the dainty fabric, and also see that they were already tight with excitement. Because just getting ready to seduce Zach was turning her on.

And she imagined he'd felt the same way last night as he'd transformed her bedroom from beach house to bordello.

Okay, now she had half of a very scanty outfit. But she needed something to wear on the lower part of her body. Of course, that could simply be her scantiest bikini panties. But she had something she thought would be much better.

As a kind of gag present when she'd started the Dear Esther column, Beth had sent her a white garter belt and white silk stockings. At the time, she'd laughed and stuffed them into a drawer. Now she pulled them out and held them up.

Feeling very decadent, she pulled off her panties and threw them on top of the knit top and bra she'd discarded. Then she fastened the garter belt around her middle, rolled the stockings up her legs and attached them to the hanging garters. It seemed indecent to wear the garter belt and stockings with nothing else on the lower part of her body. But it gave her a wicked sense of pleasure to do it anyway.

Not simply her own pleasure. She was anticipating the look on Zach's face when he saw her.

Something was missing, she decided, then realized

she needed shoes. Strappy little white high heels seemed the perfect choice.

She was already wearing the makeup she'd put on that morning. She toned it down a little, fluffed up her hair, put her discarded clothing into the closet, and lit some of the candles that still sat on the dresser.

With her preparations completed, she inspected herself in the mirror, smiling as she decided that she looked like she'd stepped out of an old-time New Orleans cathouse. The notion made her feel very naughty and very aroused.

Show time!

Clearing her throat, she walked to the door and opened it a few inches.

"Zach, can you come here for a minute?" she called out.

"What is it?" his muffled voice came from within his room.

"I need you to help me with something. In the bedroom."

"Just a minute."

She waited with her heart pounding. It felt like centuries before she heard his door open and footsteps cross the hall.

She was standing behind the door when he stepped into the room.

"Amanda?"

"Right here," she answered, pushing the door closed with the flat of one hand.

"What are you doing?"

"I guess we'll both find out."

He turned to look at her, his eyes widening as he realized she was wearing only a lacy camisole, garter belt and stockings.

Stepping to the side, she turned off the overhead light, darkening the room, except for the muted lamp in the corner and the candles.

"What are you doing?" he asked again, this time in a strangled voice.

"Hoping that turnabout is fair play. Last night you showed me one of your fantasies. I'd like to return the favor."

With more boldness than she felt, she crossed the few steps that separated them, then twined her arms around his neck and brought her face close to his, swallowing his strangled exclamation with a small kiss.

She felt his shock, and his resistance. And she wanted to pull back and say, "What's wrong? Can't you make love unless it was your idea?"

She knew those words sprang to her mind in self-defense. They came from the rawness of her own nerves.

At this moment in time, in this bedroom, he could hurt her. Not physically. She knew he would never do that. But he could deliver a crushing blow to her self-esteem. She had handed him that power.

There was a charged moment when she waited for him to pull back, open the door and walk away. But he didn't move. And she heard his breathing accelerate.

Because he was turned on?

Without giving herself time to consider the wisdom of her actions, she brushed her lips against his again. It was only the smallest part of what she wanted with him, but she felt her body heat—felt the heat coming off of him as well.

Slowly, as though they had never kissed before, she

experimented with the sensations the mouth-to-mouth contact created. Stroking him with her tongue, nibbling on his lower lip, pressing her mouth to his as she slowly increased the pressure of her flesh against his.

''Zach?'' she asked, drawing back only enough to ask the question.

He didn't answer with words, only with a sound that seemed to well up from deep in his throat as his mouth took command of her and his arms gathered her to him.

The kiss flared from hot to white-hot in the space of heartbeats. With a low growl, he angled his head, his mouth rapacious and demanding so that she needed to anchor her hands against his shoulders, press her body to his to keep from swaying on her feet.

It was like being caught in a whirlwind that spun her up and around to dizzying heights. And with her last shreds of coherence, she thought that the only hope of survival lay in clinging to Zachary Grant.

Somewhere in her disordered mind she knew that everything that had come before was only preparation for this sharp, rich moment in time. This moment and all the ones that would come after.

When he silently asked her to open her lips, she did his bidding—then shivered as his tongue took possession of her mouth.

She gave him permission to plunder. Permission to ride away with her most intimate possession—her heart. Because deep inside herself, she knew that this encounter wasn't just about sex. It was about all her tender feelings for this man that had gathered inside her.

There was not space between his body and hers, yet she inched closer, overwhelmed by the feel of his chest and hips pressed to hers. And by the erection wedged against her middle. The knowledge that she had done that to him was exhilarating.

But it wasn't enough. She wanted more.

"Zach," she murmured, nibbling her lips against his jaw as she spoke. "I love the feel of your cock. It's so nice and hard and sexy." To emphasize her words, she moved against him, pleased by the sound of his indrawn breath. "But it's kind of wasted against my stomach. So lean your hips back against the door and splay your feet out. That way I'll feel you where I need you."

For a breathless moment he looked down into her eyes. Then he did as she asked, leaning back, equalizing their heights so that his erection nestled at the top of her legs.

She moved against him, hearing her own deep sigh of satisfaction. She could come like this, she knew. Just from the friction and the sensuality.

But she didn't want it to happen yet. She wanted Zach inside her when she exploded with pleasure. So she eased a few inches back, his wordless protest giving her a kind of secret reassurance.

He'd changed when he'd gone to his room. He was wearing only a dark T-shirt, jeans and athletic socks.

Reaching out, she grabbed the hem of his T-shirt and began to roll it up, keeping her hot gaze on his as she slowly, slowly got the thin fabric out of the way—teasing them both with the languorous pace of her movements.

When she had rolled the shirt as far as she could go, she stopped to admire his chest, then leaned forward and caressed him with her face, enjoying the thick mat of his chest hair against her cheek.

Raising her hands, she found his flat nipples with her fingers. She smiled as she felt their hardness, their tightness. With her thumbs and fingers, she pulled on them, twisted them slightly, suspecting from what he'd asked her to do that he would like that.

His little exclamation told her that he did.

He had been standing with his hands at his sides. In a rush of movement, he brought them up now, capturing her hips, bringing them back against the hard shaft that strained at the front of his jeans.

She allowed him a few moments of contact before she whispered, against his ear, "Maybe it's time to get out of those pants. Aren't they feeling too tight right about now?"

He answered with an inarticulate sound.

Smiling, she put a few inches of distance between them again, then steadied her hand on his shoulder while she pulled off her white sandals and tossed them to the side.

A sharp sound pierced her consciousness. The phone. Out in the living room the phone was ringing.

She and Zach looked at each other, and she knew that neither one of them wanted to answer the damn thing. So she ignored it. The answering machine picked up, and she thought she heard Beth's voice. But she couldn't hear what her friend was saying. She didn't want to hear. She only wanted to focus on Zach.

Blocking out the message coming from the living room, she went down on her knees in front of him. When she glanced up, she saw the intensity of his expression. He looked like a man who was poised on the brink of either heaven or hell—and he didn't know which.

She was on a level with his fly. Just because she wanted to, she stroked her hand down the length of his zipper, heard the hiss of his breath as she touched him there.

Working her way back up, she unbuckled his belt, her movements as slow and deliberate as they had been when she'd rolled up his shirt.

With the buckle undone, she released the snap of his jeans, then began to inch the zipper down, feeling the tension gathering in him—and in herself.

She was so aroused she could barely stand it. But she didn't abandon her plan.

When the zipper of the jeans was fully opened, she reached inside and pulled down the front of his briefs so that she could free his cock.

It was hot and hard in her hands, and she knew it would feel exquisite inside her.

But not yet. She stroked him with her fingertips, light teasing strokes that she knew were driving him mad. Then she dragged her tongue over the length of him before circling the head with a teasing stroke.

He groaned, then groaned again when she took him in her mouth, as much of him as she could take, playing with him for a long, sensuous moment before pulling back.

Then she stood again and pulled the camisole over her head so that she was wearing only the garter belt and stockings.

"Lord, you are the sexiest sight I have ever seen," he growled. Still with his hips against the door, he pulled off his shirt and tossed it away. Then he shucked off the jeans and briefs and came toward her, catching her in his arms, bending to give her a long, deep kiss before lowering his head to capture one of her aching nipples in his mouth while he caught the other between his thumb and finger, giving her back the same pleasure she had given him—and more.

"So sexy," he said again as he reached between her legs, dipping into her hot, slick flesh.

"Oh!" She was close to orgasm, too close. "Please, Zach, I'm going to come. And I want you inside me when I do," she managed to say.

He scooped her up into his arms and carried her to the bed, laying her on the comforter and following her down.

"Now. Do it now," she gasped out, then moaned as she felt his velvet hard cock plunge inside her.

He went very still above her, then looked down into her face with an intensity that robbed her of breath.

When he began to move, she could concentrate only on the wonderful, erotic sensation of his shaft moving in and out of her.

She came then, in a wave of ecstasy that lifted her up to a high plateau and kept her suspended in the heavens.

When she drifted back to earth, he was still inside her. Still hard as a fence post. And he was staring down at her with an expression she couldn't read.

He stayed where he was, and she lifted her hand to stroke his damp shoulder, his cheek, his lips.

He kissed her fingertips.

"Zach?"

He didn't speak, only began to move his hips again, slowly and deliberately, almost withdrawing from her, then plunging back inside, building her arousal once more.

He kept the pace slow and deliberate, even when she dug her fingers into his sweat-slick shoulders, begging him to let her climax.

Not until she was thrashing wildly under him, raising her hips with each thrust, screaming silently for release did he bring her to the peak again.

This time she spun off into space, almost losing herself in the intensity of her release. But Zach was her anchor to the here and now. She clasped him by the shoulders, and when she settled back to earth, he leaned down to gently kiss the corners of her eyelids, her lips.

He stayed where he was for several heartbeats, then rolled off of her.

Turning her head, she saw him lying beside her on his back. He was breathing hard, his eyes closed, his face contorted. But it wasn't his face that captured her attention. When she looked down, she saw that he was still hard, still aroused.

What had been a fantastic experience for her had left him aching and needy.

Reaching out a hand, she laid it lightly on his shoulder.

"Zach, what can I do for you?" she asked.

13

AMANDA LAY BESIDE Zach waiting for him to say something. He didn't answer her question, only reached over the side of the bed and found the sheet she'd carefully folded. Sitting up, he flipped it open, then draped it over both of them.

It covered his nakedness—and hers. But it did little to hide the erection still sticking out from the front of his body. Instead, his rigid penis made a little tent pole for a section of the fabric.

He lay against the pillows with his eyes closed, his head turned slightly away from her.

Under the covers, she laid her hand softly over his, feeling him quiver. For a moment she stroked her fingers along his still heated skin, then said. "Zach, that was fantastic...for me."

"I'm glad," he answered, his voice barely above a whisper.

"What about you?"

He pulled his hand away. "In case you can't figure it out, I don't want to talk about me," he snapped.

"I think we should."

"Why?"

She hesitated for a moment. There were so many things she could say now. And she wasn't sure which was best. She decided on, "Because I think the two of us have gotten very close in a very short period of time. And I want to get closer. Emotionally closer.''

He made a small sound that she hoped signaled his agreement.

Turning toward him, she added, "Making love with you was wonderful for me. I see it wasn't as good for you—and I want to do something about it."

The words hung in the air between them, and she wished she hadn't spoken them.

He sat up and gave her a look that could have frozen water to ice. Punching out the words, he said, "I don't need any help from Dr. O'Neal."

Feeling at a disadvantage, she sat up, too, and pressed her palms against the comforter to keep herself from reaching for him again. A few minutes ago, they'd been as close as a man and a woman could be. Now...

"I wasn't offering help from Dr. O'Neal," she said softly.

He tipped his head to one side, studying her, and she was glad he'd found the sheet. Otherwise, she would have felt very naked.

"What were you offering?" he asked, his voice challenging her.

She gave a small shrug because she was pretty sure that if she tried to speak now, she'd start to cry.

Fighting her natural inclination to try and reach out to him with words, she pressed her lips together. Her own emotions were raw as she climbed out of bed. She had just had one of the best experiences of her life, and now she was on the edge of tears.

"Maybe it will be easier to talk when we're both dressed," she whispered, then ducked into the closet to pick up the clothing she'd discarded earlier. Wad-

ding them into a ball, she clutched them against her
chest and hurried out of the room.

To give herself something to do, she turned on the
shower and waited for the water to heat, then stepped
under the spray and just stood there for several
minutes. The hot water felt good. But not as good as
Zach's hands and lips on her. Not as good as his penis
inside her.

And hot water was certainly no substitute for a conversation with the man who had just sent her flying
off to the moon, then crashing back to earth.

While she stood under the shower spray, she fell
into the habit that had built up over the past few days.

"Dear Esther," she murmured, letting the sound of
the pounding water mask her words.

"I've met a fantastic guy. I was attracted to him
from the moment we met. I think it was the same for
him. But we started off on the wrong foot. It's complicated to explain it all. It's got to do with a murder
investigation. But that's not the important part. I can't
speak for him, but what it seems like to me is that
neither one of us wanted to walk away from the relationship."

She stopped and squeezed shampoo into her hand,
washing her hair as she continued.

"So each of us reached out to the other. I think we
both did things we wouldn't have considered with
someone else. I mean sexual things that I might have
thought of as kinky before I met him. But we did
them. And it was mind-blowing. Fantastic. Then I
wanted to just have plain old sexual intercourse. So I
seduced him. And it worked. It was just as good as I
knew it would be—right up to the end."

She turned in the spray, rinsing her hair before she went on.

"But then it all blew up in my face. I didn't satisfy him. Did I do something wrong? Or...or is there something...wrong with him?" she managed to say. "I don't like putting it in those terms. But he's not leaving me any choice, is he? Not when he's so closed up. Not when he won't talk to me.

"Can you help me, Esther?" she finished.

But she knew the only person who could help her was Zachary Grant. Unless he told her what was going on with him, they didn't have a chance.

Finally, when the water began to cool, she turned it off. Stepping out of the shower, she began to dry her body and her hair, knowing that she was drawing out the process because she didn't really want to come out of the bathroom.

But she could only spend so much time drying her hair and putting her clothes on. With a sigh, she glanced out the bathroom door. Zach wasn't around, so she went into the bedroom and retrieved her watch from the dresser.

After slipping her feet into a pair of sandals, she knew she'd stalled as long as she could. When she walked down the hall, the house felt strangely silent.

"Zach?"

She'd geared herself up for a confrontation. But he didn't answer, and when she entered the living room, she saw he'd left a note on the dining room table.

Gone for a walk.

ZACH LEANED AGAINST the low-hanging branch of a tree, looking down at the dark waters of the creek, watching them rushing over the rock and gravel that lined the streambed.

The branch swayed under his weight, but he stayed where he was.

He'd left the house because he couldn't deal with the look of disappointment on Amanda's face after they'd made love.

He'd been a damn mess since his divorce. Every sexual encounter with a woman had ended the way this one just had. He simply couldn't have an orgasm with a partner. And he'd assumed that he never would again. He knew on some level that he was punishing himself for what had happened with Mindy. But the insight hadn't changed anything.

Until he'd met Amanda—and somewhere deep inside him, hope had bloomed. Despite his previous failures, or maybe because of them, he'd taken another approach.

He'd wanted her so much. So his mind had started working on things that he could do with her that would give her satisfaction. Everything they'd done had been wonderful for him, too.

Because of her profession, he'd expected her to be sophisticated about sex. But he could tell immediately that she'd been shocked by his risqué suggestions—and by the games he'd initiated that he'd never tried with any other woman, because he hadn't cared enough to be so inventive.

She'd willingly gone along with him, though he'd sensed she wanted more. Which was why he'd been avoiding her today. But she'd taken matters into her own hands, so to speak. And she'd certainly thought of a very creative way to invite him back to her bed.

Lord, that erotic outfit she'd put together from stuff

she must have had around the house. What was she doing with a garter belt and stockings, anyway?

It didn't matter where she'd gotten them. He'd been instantly hard as a broomstick when he'd seen her looking like a cross between a convent schoolgirl and an exotic dancer. He'd wanted her so much. Wanted to please her. And there had been no way he could have refused what she was asking.

Truthfully, by the time she'd knelt down in front of him and opened his fly, he'd thought it was going to turn out okay for him—for the first time in over a year. She was so warm, and giving and sexy. And he'd been so hot, he'd thought he was going up in smoke.

But then they'd been naked in bed together, and when he'd started making love with her in the old traditional way, he'd been pretty sure it was going to end as it always did. With another woman, he might have left before the final humiliation. But not with Amanda. He cared about her too much to walk out. So he'd done the only thing he could—dedicated himself to making sure it was as good for her as possible.

His hands gripped the tree limb so fiercely that the rough bark was digging into his palms. Pushing himself away, he cursed, his angry voice ringing through the woods.

A little while ago, his own disappointment and frustration had made him lash out at Amanda—with that crack about Dr. O'Neal.

He'd seen the tears glistening in her eyes before she'd turned away. Those tears had overwhelmed him. He'd run from them, because he didn't know what else to do.

But now that he'd had time to think about it, he

knew he owed her an explanation—whatever the outcome.

He squeezed his eyes shut and clenched his hands into fists, standing there in the silence of the woods.

He didn't want to lose her. But he didn't want to live a lie with her, either. He'd said that he didn't need any help from Dr. O'Neal. But that was obviously a lie. He needed help from someone. In fact, he'd asked for her help. But not in the way he should have. Taking a deep breath and letting it out slowly, he turned and started back toward the house.

"DAMN YOU," Amanda muttered to the empty room as she stared at the words he'd scrawled in masculine handwriting across the piece of notebook paper.

"Did you realize you wrote your coward's note in the same paper you used to write that other letter— the one that led to a very erotic session in bed. When we both reached climax, then. Without touching each other."

She walked to the window and looked out, but she couldn't see him. Still, she began speaking to him again. "Doing that with you was very exciting. Partly because I'd never had a sexual encounter like that before. And partly because it was with you."

She gulped. "I don't think I could have done that with another man. Certainly not with someone I'd known for as short a time as I've known you."

"Damn you," she said again. "You can't duck away from me by going for a walk. I'll still be here when you get back. Because this relationship is too important to give up the first time we hit a problem."

She turned away from the table and saw that the light on the answering machine was blinking. It was then that she remembered someone had called while she and Zach had been getting undressed.

She even remembered who it was. Beth. And her voice had sounded urgent.

Something was wrong, and now she should deal with it.

She had just reached for the machine when the door opened.

Her heart leaped, and she looked up eagerly. But it wasn't Zach who walked inside. It was another man. A man whose face held a mixture of anger and triumph.

Instinctively she grabbed for the phone and started to dial 9-1-1. But she only got through the first two numbers before he knocked the receiver out of her hand. It clattered to the floor, sounding like thunder in the silence of the small room.

Amanda stood paralyzed by the end table, staring at the gun in the man's hand.

"What do you want?"

Long seconds passed before he answered in a low, threatening voice. "Don't you know?"

Mutely, she shook her head.

He took a half step toward her. "Well, you're going to find out. Come on."

She didn't move, couldn't move.

He took another step closer, his eyes dark and menacing, the hand with the gun jerking as it pointed at her middle. "If you don't want me to shoot you right now, turn around."

She didn't want her back to him, but she had no doubt that if she tried to make a run for it, he would do what he said. So she turned. In the next moment, she felt cold metal click over her wrists. Handcuffs.

He'd come prepared to restrain her.

When her hands were secured, he spun her around to face the door.

"We'd better get going before lover boy comes back and I have to shoot him. You wouldn't want to get him killed would you?"

Amanda's gasp made the man grin. Then his fingers closed around her arm, and he was hurrying her out the door. Down the driveway she saw a white van.

Zach had told her a man with a white van had been hanging around her house. He'd broken in, but Zach had chased him away. Now he was back. Somehow he'd figured out where they were hiding.

She stumbled, thinking that if she fell to the ground, he'd have to carry her, and that might slow him down.

But he was apparently prepared for the maneuver.

"No you don't," he growled, jerking her up painfully by her arms and dragging her toward the vehicle. He was making no attempt to be gentle, and she knew that if she resisted, he'd likely yank her shoulder out of joint.

"No. Please. Let me go. What have I done to you?" she pleaded, hearing the terror in her own voice, and hating herself for being on the edge of hysteria.

"Not to me. To other people."

'What?"

"Shut up. Just shut up."

There was a menacing note in his voice that made her press her lips closed. This man was angry—and unbalanced. And she'd better go along with him quietly.

Yanking the side door of the van open, he shoved

her inside. She made a small sound of protest when she saw that a length of chain was dangling from the armrest of the seat closest to the door. He used the chain to secure her handcuffs to the armrest so she couldn't lean fully against the seat back. When she was secure, he slammed the door closed and went around to the driver's side.

Moments later, he was speeding down the drive-way.

JUST AS HE EMERGED from the woods, Zach saw a white van. It was heading away from the house, picking up speed as it went. But he could see Amanda's blond head through one of the windows.

''God, no!'

With a curse of anger and fear, he ran to his own car, but he hadn't been planning for a quick getaway when he'd pulled in. He'd thought they were safe in this house, so he was facing in the wrong direction.

By the time he backed down the drive, the van was nowhere in sight, and he had to choose which way to go when he reached the highway. A stream of traffic was coming from the left, in the direction of town, so he went right—partly because it seemed logical that the guy wouldn't be heading into the country. But although he floored the gas pedal, he didn't catch up with the van. Which probably meant he was going in the wrong direction.

Or was he? There was no way to tell when he was driving blind. He needed help.

Still, he sped on for another few miles, his curses filling the interior of his car.

The bastard had gotten to Amanda. And it was his own damn fault. Somehow the guy who'd been after her had figured out where they were staying. Then he had taken a chance on snatching her up when he'd known she was alone in the house.

Zach cursed again.

His own damn inadequacies had sent him slinking out of the house while Amanda was in the shower because he didn't want to have a conversation about himself. But if he'd only had the guts to stick around to face her, she'd be safe.

Blind fear had sent him charging after her. Now he admitted he was wasting time driving around looking for her—when he'd obviously lost the van. Fighting the sick feeling rising in his throat, he pulled onto a side road, made a U-turn in a driveway, and went speeding back the way he'd come.

When he reached the house, he jumped out of the car and raced toward the door. It was open, and he leaped inside, then sped around the interior.

The phone receiver was lying on the floor, and he picked it up. And the light on the answering machine was blinking. He remembered then that Amanda had gotten a call while they'd been in the bedroom.

He didn't want to take the time to get the message. But his training told him it could be important. So he pressed the button.

"Amanda? Amanda, pick up, damn you."

He recognized Beth Cantro's voice. She was the editor he'd interviewed in New York before coming down here.

"Amanda, I have some information for you. About Esther. The police found the car that hit her. It's a long story. It belongs to a guy named Tony Anderson. He didn't answer his phone for over a week, so his sister had the authorities investigate. There was a car locked in his garage—with blood on the bumper. The police did some checking, and they found that it was Esther's blood. Amanda, he may be after you. Please give that information to Zachary. And please call me back as soon as you can. I'm so worried.''

Jesus! Zach stood staring at the machine.

So a guy named Tony Anderson was the one after Amanda. But what good was the information going to do him now?

His mind raced, sorting through facts, making connections. If it was the same guy, he'd deliberately plowed down Esther in the street. But from the start, his goals had been different with Amanda. He'd been in a hurry to eliminate Esther from the planet. But he'd been stalking Amanda. He could have killed her days ago, if he'd wanted to. Which meant he was interested in her in a different way. He'd wanted to keep her alive. For a while. At least that's what Zach hoped to hell was true.

Striding toward his room, he picked up a piece of electronic equipment that he'd left sitting on the dresser.

AMANDA HUDDLED on the bench seat of the white van, shifting to get a little more comfortable. Was there some way to free herself? Working as quietly as she could, she tried to remove the metal chain from the armrest.

A voice cut through her concentration. ''Don't bother,'' he said, sounding almost bored. ''What do you think? That I'm stupid enough to let you get away now that I have you where I want you?''

''No,'' she answered automatically.

He laughed. ''Right. Try to give the man the correct answer. Well, the correct answer is that you need a hacksaw—or the key—to get out of that thing.''

She kept her head down, cringing away from the grating quality of his voice. She wanted to block him out, to disappear into her own mind. Or into a fantasy. She kept picturing Zachary pulling up beside the van, ramming it with his car, forcing the kidnapper to stop. Then he'd get her out of here and take her in his arms, and everything would be all right again.

Zach. Oh Lord, Zach, she silently whispered. But as much as she wanted him to come charging to her rescue, she knew it wasn't going to happen. He didn't even realize she was missing; and if he did, he wouldn't have a clue where she had gone—or why.

He'd stomped out of the house to go for a walk. He'd been angry. And probably he'd jump to the conclusion that she was angry, too—that she'd run out on him. Oh God, she didn't want him to think that. Because she wasn't going to let him go that easily. She would stay and fight for the two of them.

She smiled, feeling her own resolve building. She wanted to keep thinking about him. About their relationship. About what they could mean to each other if he'd only drop his iron barriers. She would make him let her get close to him. Really close.

But she knew all that was just a comforting daydream. Thinking about Zachary Grant wasn't going to do anything for her at the present moment. She was with another man, a man who was going to do something terrible to her—unless she could talk him out of it. Which she had a good chance of doing, she told herself. Because she understood people and their motivations.

The pep talk helped. Sitting up straighter, she

looked toward the front of the van, then cleared her throat. "What do you want with me?" she asked.

He kept her waiting for several agonizing seconds before answering, "You'll find out."

"You were stalking me," she heard herself say and instantly regretted the observation. What good did it do to point out the obvious? Maybe he'd resent having a label put on his behavior.

He answered in a casual voice. Too casual. "If that's what you want to call it. To me, it was more like a stakeout. Like the police do when they're after a criminal."

A criminal? Was that how he saw her? Well, it fit with the way he'd hauled her off in handcuffs. He was going to punish her. But for what?

Wanting to keep him talking, she asked, "At least tell me why you took me away."

"Because you had the arrogance to step into Esther Knight's shoes," he spat out, and now she felt his anger building. "You're going to be Esther Scott, and you deserve the same punishment that she got. More punishment, actually."

She didn't want him to focus on punishment, so she changed the subject abruptly. "What did I do to you?"

"You think you have all the answers."

"No. If I thought I had all the answers, I wouldn't be asking questions."

Ignoring her, he plowed on. "Yeah, you do. You're like her. My girlfriend wrote Esther Knight a letter, and she answered her. And Vicki left me."

"That's not my fault," she tried again.

He wasn't listening to her. Instead he began to re-

cite in a singsong voice, a letter he had obviously
memorized:

"Dear Esther, I have a problem, and I need help.
My boyfriend and I have been together for several
months. At first he was really great. He worked really
hard to get me to be his girlfriend. He was so atten-
tive. He wrote me poetry. He bought me little presents
all the time."

The man in the front seat turned and glared at
Amanda before directing his attention back to the
road.

"But now I'm starting to be afraid of him. He
wants to control everything in my life. He made me
quit my job, because he says he can take care of me.
So I have lots of time on my hands. But he doesn't
let me go shopping, and he doesn't let me see my
friends. And we only see my parents when he's with
me. When we're in bed together, he wants to tie me
up and do things to me I don't like. Please tell me
how to get away from him. Signed, Desperate in New
York."

The man turned again, his angry gaze drilling into
her. "What do you think of that?"

"I—" she said but couldn't get any further.

"Speak up," he snapped. "I want to hear what you
have to say about it."

This guy was angry. Out of control. And she recognized that whatever she said was going to be
wrong.

She sat there paralyzed as he went on.

"I'll tell you the crappy advice Esther gave
Vicki... 'Dear Desperate, you have to get away from
this man. He sounds dangerous. There are shelters for
abused women. The next time you are alone in the

house, walk away. If there's no time to pack, leave your clothing and everything else. Go to a relative or friend you trust. Don't let this man destroy your life'," he ended with a sound that was a cross between a growl and a curse.

"And she did just what Esther told her. She left everything and ran away. The magazine was open on the kitchen table so I could see where she'd gotten the nerve to go against me. And she left me a note saying she was sorry. She said she was going to some shelter where I couldn't find her. She must have started planning it in secret. Then she waited for her chance and left. Do you know how mad that made me?" he snarled.

"Yes," she answered because she heard the fury in his voice. And she shuddered, because she knew that the only one he could take it out on was her. His girlfriend was gone. Esther was gone. Now there was only her to stand in for both of them and take the heat.

He was on a roll now, speaking as if he didn't care who was listening, because he just wanted to get the story out. It had been bottled up inside of him for months, and he'd had no one he could tell. Now he literally had a captive audience.

"Vicki thought she could get away from me, Tony Anderson. I looked all over for her, you know. I'm still looking for her. She may be hidden now. But she's going to mess up. And when I find her, I'm going to make her sorry she left. I haven't given up.

"But meanwhile, I figured out how to find that bitch, Esther Knight. It was supposed to be a secret who she was, but I got a line on her through the magazine. See, the letters come to them, and they send them on to Esther.'' He laughed. ''Simple, if you know how to figure things out.''

When he looked at her in the rearview mirror again, his eyes had narrowed to slits. ''I thought it was all over when I killed her. I felt really happy. I thought she wouldn't ruin anyone else's life. But the columns were still being printed, and I realized that they'd been written a couple months in advance. I kept checking the mail room again, just to make sure it was all over. But it wasn't. The letters kept coming, and I found out there was a new person writing the Esther Scott column. You,'' he said, the sentence ending in a snarl.

''I've watched you reading letters. I've watched you sitting at your laptop—making up nasty answers. But your column's never going to be finished, and it's never going to be printed. If some fool is arrogant enough to take it over, then I'll do to her what I'm going to do to you. And if your dear friend Beth doesn't get the picture, then I'll have to take care of her, too.''

Amanda sat there with her heart pounding. Unable to look at the man behind the wheel, she stared at the scenery flying past. Houses. Trees. Billboards.

She could follow the route because he wasn't making any attempt to hide where they were going.

Either he'd made some terrible mistakes, or he didn't expect her to lead anyone to the place where he'd taken her—because she'd be dead when their time together was finished.

A surge of black fear threatened to sweep her under, like a merciless riptide. She didn't want to know what he had planned for her, but she suspected she was going to find out soon enough.

14

ZACHARY STOOD in the middle of the empty bedroom. Not the one where he and Amanda had made love. The other bedroom—where he'd planned to sleep.

He barely saw the room now. He felt like he was in the middle of a forest fire. At least he felt like his head was filling up with smoke and every breath seared his lungs.

It had been a long time since he had asked for divine help. Now he said a silent prayer.

"Please God, let me find Amanda. If something happens to her because I ran out on her, I'll never forgive myself."

His jaw clenched when he realized what he'd just said. So he started again. "Please God, let me find Amanda. She's a good woman. Caring. Loving. She can help so many people. If you just let me save her."

That was the best he could do in the prayer department, he thought as his surroundings blinked back into focus. Turning toward the dresser, he picked up the piece of electronic equipment he'd set on top. Then he turned a switch to "on," his whole body vibrating with tension as the small display screen lit up.

He breathed out a sigh of relief when he saw the bull's eye in the center. A light was blinking on the screen, and he watched it move toward the ten o'clock position.

Close to the edge. He'd better hurry if he was going to keep up with the damn thing.

Yesterday, when he'd been out, he'd invested in this electronic surveillance system, thinking that he was taking the precaution "just in case" the worst happened.

While Amanda had been in the shower, he'd attached a transponder to her watch without telling her what he was doing, because he hadn't wanted to worry her.

He'd thought he was being overcautious. Now he was damn glad that he'd had the foresight to tag her. Because it meant he could find her.

After snapping a clip into his gun and stowing a spare in his pocket, he picked up the signal box and left the house.

Slipping behind the wheel of his car, he set the box on the seat beside him, then roared out of the driveway. He'd never used an electronic tracking system before, and it took him a little time to get used to it.

Precious time.

But he'd read the directions.

When Amanda's signal slipped off the edge of the screen, he filled the interior of the car with curses and pressed the gas pedal to the floor.

Then he told himself to calm down and think. He could do this!

A horn honked, and he realized he was drifting toward the wrong side of the road.

Damn! He pulled onto the shoulder, raising a cloud of gravel as his wheels spun to a stop. Picking up the box, he got her signal back by adjusting the range to cast a wider net. The blip came back on the screen, fainter, but there. So he started up again, and got back into better range before going back to the more local setting.

As he drove, he tried to send his thoughts to Amanda. He knew it was irrational, but it helped him stay calm to feel like he was communicating with her. Maybe it was even doing some good.

"Amanda, you're a smart woman. You understand people. And you're a psychologist. Deal with this guy. Don't let him hurt you. Do whatever it takes to stay alive."

Did she even know what the SOB wanted? Or who he was?

"I'm so sorry," he said aloud, speaking to Amanda again. "I came down here to investigate a murder, and it looks like I didn't do my job."

Of course, sorry wasn't going to cut it. He had to catch up with her. He had to get there before she got hurt. Or...

He couldn't deal with "or." So he wrapped his hands around the steering wheel, unconsciously hunching forward as he kept driving.

The trail led him out onto the highway, then away from St. Stephens into a rural area.

Was he taking her to the woods? Or to a house? He hoped it was the latter, for a lot of reasons.

The man named Tony Anderson drove slowly into the woods. It was dark and shadowy under the canopy of branches, making Amanda feel even more alone and isolated—with a madman.

Still, she found herself wishing that the narrow road

would keep going on forever. And that he would forget all about the woman in the backseat.

But she knew the journey was going to come to an end, and soon enough she saw lights through the trees. The shadowy bulk of a house loomed in the forest. Pulling to a stop, he cut the engine.

"End of the line," he said, the words sending shivers down her spine.

She wanted to beg him to let her go, but she knew it wouldn't do any good, so she choked back the plea as he held the gun on her with one hand and used the other to unlock the chain that secured her to the armrest.

She thought about trying to slam the metal cuffs on her wrists into his face but finally decided that she'd only end up getting shot for her efforts.

"Let's go. Move."

She got up stiffly, and he gave her a shove toward the door of the van.

"Into the house. The door is unlocked. Open it."

Awkwardly, she twisted the knob and stepped inside—and found herself in a brightly lit room. There was almost no furniture, just a big, bare space with one chair and one table.

He marched her across to the far wall, pulled her arms above her head, and clicked another chain into place. All of it happened so quickly that she didn't have time to formulate an escape plan.

Stepping back, he carefully set his gun down on the table, then slowly raised his eyes to hers. The way his gaze traveled over her body made her want to scream, but she managed to keep her lips pressed together, because she wasn't going to give him the satisfaction of seeing her turn to jelly. That was what he wanted, and she could keep that much from him.

Or was that the wrong approach? Would it be better to scream and cower? Which strategy would keep her alive longer?

She was trained in psychology. She should know what to do, but she could hardly make her brain function.

His lips moved, and she realized he was speaking.

"You know, I had a lot of time to think about the best way to punish you," he said in a conversational voice. "And what I decided was that since you presumed to give other women sexual advice, we should make this a sexual adventure together. I think we're going to have a lot of fun playing out some of my most vivid fantasies. At least I am."

He came closer, and her fear leaped up, making her lose control so that she kicked out at him with her left foot. But he must have been waiting for some show of aggression, because he danced back—out of the way.

"Resistance is futile," he said, then slapped her hard across the face. "You know, like the Borg say on *Star Trek*." He laughed at his own joke.

"But let's make sure you can't do that again." While she was still smarting from the slap, he quickly knelt and secured her ankles to cuffs near the floor.

"Now we'll get started." He stepped back and looked at her. "Tell me why you took the job as Esther Scott."

Okay. He wanted to talk. Keep him talking, she thought. The longer he talks, the better.

"My friend, Beth Cantro, needed someone to fill in."

"Are you saying you never intended to make the job permanent?"

What was the right answer? Amanda licked her lips. "I hadn't made that decision yet," she finally temporized.

"I'm going to make it for you." When he pulled out a knife, she made a strangled sound of fear.

He answered with a knowing smile.

WHEN THE DOT stopped moving and stayed in the same position for over two minutes, Zach banged his hands against the wheel. The bastard had arrived at his destination—and that was both good and bad.

Finding Tony Anderson was going to be a sure thing. But it also meant that he'd taken Amanda to where he intended to deal with her.

He could kill her now. But Zach was praying he wasn't going to do that yet. He could have killed her at home, but he'd chosen to cart her away. Where he could have what he undoubtedly thought was quality time with her.

He made a low sound that was equal parts fear and anger. His foot pressed down on the accelerator. When he overshot the driveway, he had to double back.

The narrow lane led onto a rural property—and straight toward the green dot on the screen. Zach wanted to roar up the road and mow the guy down with his vehicle. But he wasn't some kind of comic book superhero. So he pulled to a stop in a patch of weeds and jumped out, making his way on foot. The guy could have alarms out, but most likely he was too sure of himself to think he needed protection.

Rounding a curve, through the trees he saw the

silhouette of a house. The lights were on, shining out like a beacon into the night and, as he drew closer, he saw a white van parked up front.

It flashed through his mind that calling the cops was a definite option now. He knew from the transponder that Amanda was here, and he might need some help.

The trouble was, he'd seen small-town police departments in action. In a crisis, they tended to go for their guns, and Amanda could get caught in the cross fire.

So, for the moment, he figured he was better off on his own.

Weapon drawn, his pulse pounding in his ears, he crept up to one of the windows and peeked inside. What he saw made the blood in his veins turn to ice.

His gaze zeroed in on Amanda. She was chained to a wall, her face a mask of fear. And the bastard was standing over her, cutting off her clothing with a hunting knife. He'd cut her shirt off. As Zach watched, he slashed through first one bra strap and then the other. After yanking down the cups and exposing her breasts, he cut the fabric at the front of the garment, then lifted it away from her before tossing it onto the floor.

The breath solidified in Zach's lungs. Every instinct made him want to burst through the door and go for the bastard. But not when he was cutting with that knife.

As he evaluated the situation, Zach decided it didn't look like Anderson was planning to murder her right away. It looked like he was planning to terrify her first.

And sick as that thought made Zach, he also knew it bought him some time.

Her fear tore at him. He wanted to press his face against the window, so that Amanda could see him. He wanted her to know that she wasn't alone, and he was going to rescue her. But he understood that revealing his presence wasn't a good idea. If she saw him, the look on her face would change, and that would give too much away. Edging closer, he tried to hear what was going on inside.

"Write me a letter," the guy was saying. "I want to hear what advice you'd give to Vicki."

Amanda licked her lips. "I don't know."

"Talk!"

"I…I would tell her that she should evaluate her options," she stammered. "She shouldn't act hastily."

"You're lying. You're saying what you think I want to hear." As he spoke, Anderson raised his hand and slapped her.

Through the glass, he heard her breath catch. But she didn't scream.

Zach made himself stay in place.

Now he was wondering if he'd made the wrong decision. If he met the cops at the end of the road, he could help them keep their cool. The problem was, he might not have time.

As he watched, Anderson slid his hand down her naked belly and inside the waistband of her slacks.

The intimate touch of those fingers on Amanda's flesh was more than Zach could stand. He had to get her out of there before the sicko inflicted any more psychological damage.

Slowly he twisted the knob and found the door unlocked. Taking a calculated risk that the guy would leap to defend himself, Zach eased the door open a fraction of an inch, then kicked it inward with his foot. Almost in the same moment, he jumped out of the way so that he could look around the edge of the window.

Through the glass he saw Anderson whirl away from Amanda, grab his gun from the table, and fire at the door.

In old Westerns, the guys holed up in the house broke out the glass in the windows with the butts of their guns before firing. Zach knew that step wasn't necessary. The glass wasn't going to slow a bullet from a large-caliber gun like his or change the trajectory.

Raising his weapon, he fired through the window, dodging flying shards of glass, seeing Anderson stagger.

Amanda screamed, and the bastard half turned back toward her.

God no! He silently screamed as he kept firing until the kidnapper dropped to the floor and lay unmoving.

Then he burst through the door.

Amanda stared at him, wide-eyed. "Zach," she gasped.

"It's all right. Everything's all right. He can't hurt you anymore. Just hang on a second," he shouted, then knelt over Anderson, who was still holding his revolver. And there was a spray of bullets in the door and the wall. So, when the cops arrived, there would be no doubt what had happened here.

When he detected no pulse in the man's neck, he felt through his pockets and located a set of keys.

Standing, he set his weapon on the table in full

view, before hurrying to Amanda. She was staring at him with large blue eyes, and he couldn't deal with the fear and pain he saw there. Quickly he knelt to free her ankles. Then he placed his own body between hers and the thug on the floor while he worked at the chain that held her wrists. When he'd freed her, she sagged into his arms and started to sob.

"It's all right. You're all right. He won't hurt you again," he murmured, as he stroked his hands over her back and into her hair.

She continued to cry, but he felt her nod against his shoulder. He wanted her out of the house—away from the horror of what had happened and away from Anderson's body.

Picking her up, he cradled her tenderly in his arms, then carried her out the door and to his car. He opened the passenger door and eased her into the seat, careful of her head as he held her to him and rocked her in his arms, stroked her, giving himself over to a profound sense of relief. And also regret. Because he'd screwed up again. He'd let this happen to her.

"You're all right," he repeated, hoping to God it was true.

She was trembling in his arms, but he could tell she was trying to get herself under control. Finally she sucked in a shaky breath. "I'm all right because you got here in time."

"You kept yourself alive."

"I didn't do much. He was so angry. He wouldn't listen to anything I had to say."

All he could do was hold her, comfort her, pray that she was going to recover quickly from the trauma.

Raising her face, she looked into his eyes, and he

braced for a barrage of accusations. He felt like he'd been given a reprieve when she said, "I thought I was on my own. How did you know where to find me?"

"I put a tracker on your watch."

"A what?"

"A transponder that sent out a signal. At the time I thought I was being overcautious. Then I was damn glad I did it."

"Yes. And I'm damn glad I put it on."

His fingers closed around her shoulders. "Are you all right?"

"Yes."

She was still shaking, and he knew she was contemplating her close call. But she was alive, and he knew she was resilient. She'd recover—better than Mindy had. At least he could content himself with that.

"He...he killed Esther."

"I know. You had a phone message from Beth Cantro, warning you about him."

"Beth called?"

"Yes, that was the phone call we didn't answer," he said, his voice tense. Another bad mistake he'd made.

Amanda gave a quick nod. "He told me why he killed her. His girlfriend wrote Esther a letter about her boyfriend, and Esther advised her to ditch him. She did, and he was out for revenge. Then he found the column was still continuing. So he went after the person who was writing it now." She shuddered.

He pulled her closer. "It's all over. But I've got to call the cops."

She blinked, then looked down at her chest. "I'm half-naked."

"You can wear my jacket." Glad he could do something else for her, he eased away, shrugged out of the garment, and helped her get her arms through the sleeves. Then he pulled the front over her breasts and zipped the zipper.

"Better?" he asked.

"A little."

He cleared his throat. "When the cops come, you'll need to tell them what happened. How he took you away. And…uh…you saw that he fired first, right?"

She nodded, then sat up straighter. "Yes, I'm perfectly clear on that. You made a noise at the door and drew his fire. He started shooting, and you fired back."

"Yes."

Still holding her, he got out his cell phone and called the local cops and told them what had happened.

Then he sat back and hugged her to him, thinking how lucky he was to still have her in his arms. When she got over the shock, she was going to remember that she'd gotten captured by Anderson because Zachary Grant had walked out of the house and left her alone.

15

FOR AMANDA, the next few hours passed in a blur. The St. Stephens cops called the state police, who arrived and inspected the crime scene. Then she and Zach each told what had happened.

After that, they had to go down to the police barracks and make formal statements. Zach shepherded her through the process, but she sensed that he was distancing himself from her.

On the way home, he hardly said a word to her. She slid him a sideways glance, wanting to stretch out her hand and lay it over his. But she didn't, because she felt like she couldn't reach him. Not now.

She wasn't sure how long he'd been standing at the window watching her and Tony Anderson. But she knew he'd seen some of what the stalker had done to her. And she knew there were men who would react very negatively to that. They wouldn't want a relationship with a woman who'd been mauled by someone else—even if it wasn't her fault.

She knew she and Zach needed to talk, but every time she tried to think of what to say, the words froze in her throat.

He pulled up at the house. They got out of the car, then stood awkwardly in the middle of the kitchen.

She couldn't deal with the look of tension on his

face, so she said, "I think maybe I'd like to take a shower."

"I understand," he said stiffly. "But Beth called. She was worried about you, and you should tell her you're okay."

"Lord, I forgot all about her. Of course, you're right." Rushing to the phone, she dialed her friend's home number.

Beth answered on the first ring. "Amanda! I've been sitting by the phone, hoping you'd call. Did you get my message? Are you all right?"

"I'm fine." She sucked in a breath and let it out, wondering how much to say. Then she realized that it was probably going to make the papers in New York, since Esther was from there. "Now, don't get worried," she said.

"Amanda, what happened?"

"That guy—Tony Anderson—he came after me. But…but Zach rescued me."

He was standing to her right, and she could see his face contort, but he said nothing.

"Where's Anderson? Is he still a threat?" Beth asked.

"Zach shot him. He's dead."

As she heard the strangled exclamation on the other end of the line, she sank down onto one of the bar stools at the kitchen counter. "It's okay. Honest, it worked out okay."

"Were you there when…when it happened?"

"Yes."

"Oh my God. I got you into this, didn't I?"

"Beth, it is not your fault," she responded, and then launched into an explanation of what had happened.

It took twenty minutes to reassure her friend. And she had to make a promise that she'd call the next day.

"You look exhausted," Zach said when she got off the phone.

"We'll talk later," she answered in a weary voice, then headed toward the bathroom.

She had used up all her emotional energy for the moment, and she wanted to be alone. She didn't want any surprises, so she locked the door. After turning on the water in the shower, she stripped off her clothing, then stepped under the spray—turning it up as hot as she could stand.

She stayed under the pounding water for a long time, soaping herself—then doing it again, trying to wash away the feel of Tony Anderson's hands on her body. She knew the need was irrational. He was dead. And really, he'd hardly done anything to her, compared to what she knew could have happened. Compared to what she knew had been done to other women. But she couldn't stifle the need to cleanse herself.

When she was finally ready to emerge from the bathroom, she slipped into the terry cloth robe she'd left on the back of the door and stood with her hand on the knob for a moment. Maybe she'd misread Zach. Maybe he was thinking he should give her some space. Maybe she should get dressed and go look for him.

Going to her bedroom, she stopped short in the doorway.

She'd had an image of the room in her mind. The love cave that Zach had created for their mutual pleasure. But while she'd been in the bathroom, he had apparently been working at lightning speed to destroy that image.

He'd put the room back the way it had been before he'd first transformed it. The bed was up on its frame again—with the previous bedspread in place. The dresser was pushed against the wall. The candles were gone.

She stood staring at the transformation. Why had he done it? Because he thought she'd be more comfortable? Or was he trying to wipe away the memory that they'd made love here?

She felt too shaky to face him at the moment, not when tears were welling in her eyes. She was too fragile to take his rejection.

Then she firmed her lips. She was no coward. She wasn't going to hide from him and hide from herself.

If he was going to walk away from her, she wanted to find out—now. But when she strode into the living room, he wasn't there, and panic rose in her throat.

He wouldn't just leave—without saying goodbye, would he?

Her stomach knotted as she spotted his luggage sitting beside the couch. While she stood uncertainly in the middle of the floor, the back door opened, and he stepped into the kitchen.

His eyes met hers, and they both stood for a frozen moment, neither of them speaking.

She was the one who broke the silence with a sharp question. "What are you doing?"

"Getting out of your hair."

"Were you going to leave without saying goodbye?"

"I was going to write you a note—if you weren't out before I finished getting ready."

The coward's way out, she thought. But she kept that opinion to herself. She'd worked up the courage to come out here. Apparently he wasn't prepared to give her the same courtesy.

"Why did you put my room back the way it was?"

"I thought you'd want me to clear out," he said, sounding defensive.

"I think you could let me make that decision," she answered, hating the strident note in her voice. It had been less than a week since this man had walked into her life, but she'd thought something important was happening between them. Now she was struggling with the crushing disappointment that it had just been wishful thinking.

Still, she wasn't going to just let him slink away. She was going to make him tell her what he was feeling—no matter how much it hurt.

"Why are you leaving?" she asked, struggling to hold her voice steady.

He ran his hand through his hair in a quick, uneasy gesture. That small sign gave her a kernel of hope that he wasn't as indifferent as he'd sounded. "Isn't it obvious?" he said.

"Not to me," she managed to say. "I'd like you to explain."

His face turned hard. "All right. If you need to hear me state the obvious. You were kidnapped, and it was my damn fault. I left you alone when I should have been here. I understand why you don't want to have anything more to do with me."

"What?" she gasped, hardly able to believe what she'd just heard.

"I was stupid enough to make the same mistake twice. I told you, a kidnapper came after my wife because of a case I was on. I vowed I wasn't going to let anything happen to you. But that's not the way it turned out.''

Suddenly, she had a lot better idea of what was going on in his mind. ''Your wife left you,'' she said softly.

''That's right.''

''And you assumed I was going to react the way she did. So you were walking out before I could tell you to leave.''

''Yeah.''

''And that's why you put the bedroom back the way it was. You were erasing your presence from the house.''

He sighed.

''You know, when people don't communicate with each other, some whopping misunderstandings can result,'' she said in an even voice. ''You were acting so cold and distant. And from my point of view, it looked like you were leaving because you couldn't stand the thought of being with a woman who was damaged goods.''

''What the hell are you talking about?''

''There are plenty of men who can't cope with the idea that someone else touched their lover. So they emotionally withdraw.''

''You think I'm that kind of jerk?''

''The way you were acting, you didn't leave me much choice.''

''I was getting out of your way.''

''You were running away so I couldn't hurt you—the way your wife did,'' she corrected him.

He didn't deny it, only shifted his weight from one foot to the other.

"Zach, I think we need to talk. If you're willing to talk, that is," she added, holding her breath as she waited for his answer.

She saw him swallow. "All right."

She'd boldly started this conversation. Now she felt her own mouth go dry as she turned toward the seating area and lowered herself into the wingback chair.

When she found she was gripping the padded arms, she clasped her hands in her lap. She was very conscious that she'd rushed out here in her robe—with nothing under it. Now she wished she'd taken the time to get dressed. Only if she'd done that, maybe Zach would have already gone—and she would have lost this chance.

Chance—for what? Despite her resolve to remain calm, she found that her heart was racing.

When he looked expectantly at her, she licked her dry lips, then said, "If you assumed I blamed you, you're wrong."

"I left you alone in the house."

"You obviously thought we were safe here."

"I obviously made a miscalculation!"

"Stop it!"

"Stop what?"

"Putting up barriers between us." When she saw he was about to speak again, she rushed on. "I'm not your former wife. I know you wouldn't have deliberately put me in jeopardy. The most thankful moment of my life was when I knew you'd come to rescue me. Zach, I know you could have gotten yourself killed. I know what kind of risk you were taking."

"I owed you that much."

"You don't *owe* me anything. I don't want anything from you that you're not freely willing to give."

He sat on the sofa, regarding her, his hands pressed to the cushions as though he needed to ground himself.

There was so much she wanted to make him understand, and she didn't know where to start. But she knew the important thing: that he needed to believe what she was saying.

"Your wife was looking for someone to blame for her own inadequacies. So she took it out on you," she said softly.

"What are you talking about?"

"Well, speaking as a trained psychologist," she began, because she thought that might give her observations more weight, "all marriages go through ups and downs. If the people care enough about each other to make it work, they stay together. If one of them doesn't, then it's not going to survive, no matter how much the other partner wants to keep the relationship going."

She saw he was listening closely.

"I'd say you already had problems, and she used the kidnapping as an excuse to leave you."

He would have never reached that conclusion on his own. It seemed he felt too guilty about what had happened a year ago, and that guilt had spilled over into her relationship with him.

"I think she made you feel that you weren't worth being loved," she said softly, wanting to say still more, yet reluctant to put too many ideas into his head.

Neither of them spoke for several moments, and

she watched him comb his fingers against the sofa
cushions. Finally, he cleared his throat.

"After...after you and I made love, I left the house
because I didn't want...to explain what's wrong with
me."

She wanted to shout that nothing was wrong, and
if there was, they could work it out together. But she
kept her lips pressed together.

"Just before Anderson hustled you out of the
house, I was coming back to tell you about it."

She felt simultaneously elated and fearful. "What
did you want to say?" she managed to ask.

"It's not that easy to talk about."

"I know," she whispered. "But maybe I can make
it a little easier." Climbing out of the chair, she
crossed the room and lowered herself to the sofa, so
that she was sitting beside him, but not with her back
against the sofa cushions. Instead she swung around
so that she was facing him. Leaning forward, she
slung her arms around him and laid her head on his
shoulder. For heartbeats, he sat stiffly. Then he
clasped her to him.

They held each other for long moments before she
murmured, "There's nothing you can tell me that I
haven't heard before."

"Oh yeah? You mean—like a guy who can't reach
climax when he's with a woman?" he asked in a
gritty voice. "I mean a guy who can do it by himself
but not with a partner."

She had suspected that might be what he was going
to say. Keeping her own voice low and even, she
asked, "And that's been true since your wife pinned
the kidnapping rap on you?"

"Yeah."

Raising her head, she looked him in the eye. "But you wanted to get close to me—so you came up with all kinds of nice inventive ways to get around the problem. Very arousing ways."

She saw him swallow. "But you wanted more than that," he said. "You deserve more than that."

"Zach, I loved everything we did together. You are a very sexy man, whether you think so or not. You knew how to give a woman great pleasure with your hands and mouth. And you can make me go up in smoke just by talking sexy to me on the phone. But I'd be lying if I said I didn't want to have intercourse with you—that I didn't want us to both climax that way."

"And what if I can't?"

"I believe you can," she answered, thinking that his problem was going to make it tough to have his children. But she didn't say that, because it would be giving too much away.

"It's been almost a year since I could..." He stopped and clenched his jaw. "Since I could function normally."

"Don't put it that way."

"How would Dr. O'Neal put it?"

She gave a little shrug. "You know how shrinks are. They don't give opinions lightly."

He laughed, then sobered again. "Okay, you can call it anything you like. I want you right now. Just holding you and knowing that you're naked under that robe is making me so hard I can barely sit still. But I'm afraid that if we went down the hall to the bedroom, it would end up the same way it did last night."

"I'm not suggesting that we go down the hall right now. Dr. O'Neal has a more inventive prescription."

He raised one eyebrow. "And just what would Dr. O'Neal suggest?"

She leaned back and gave him a sweet smile, drawing out the moment before answering. "Well, for starters. I'd ask you to unpack your bags. Or I'd pack mine. Because I can write the column anywhere, and we don't have to stay here. We can go to New Jersey so you can get back to work. I can stay with you, but we won't try to make love. Not for a while. We'll get to know each other better. But we won't do anything that leads to sexual satisfaction. We'll wait on that until we're both so hot that we're close to spontaneous combustion."

"You'd do that for me?"

"Yes."

"Why?"

She didn't want to give away the whole show. So she simply said, "Because I think you and I are very good together. I don't want to give that up." Before he could press her, she hurried on. "Will you try what I'm suggesting?" she asked, holding her breath as she waited for his answer.

He met her steady gaze. The word "yes," came out as a low rumble in his chest.

She let out the breath she'd been unconsciously holding. "Where do you want to stay? Down here? Or should we go back north?"

"Back home. So I can return to work. I'm in Paramus. Where the mortgage payments are lower."

"Okay. We'll go up there. Then you'll have something to do during the day besides sit around staring at me."

Leaning over, she sealed the bargain with a kiss. A kiss that she intended to keep light. But it flared up like a match set to dry tinder—leaving them both breathless and shaky.

And leaving her wondering just how long she was going to be able to keep herself from dragging him to bed.

16

AMANDA LEANED BACK in the leather chair across
from Beth Cantro. She was pleased with her first Esther Scott column, and she'd come into town to deliver it in person.

Part of her reasoning had been to get out of the
house, because living within those four walls was getting a little tense. It had been only five days since
she'd made her pact with Zach, and she was already
wondering how long she could possibly hold out.

As if Beth knew the woman across the desk was a
bundle of sexual frustration, she gave her a considering look. "You seem kind of...on edge," she said.
"When you told me you were back up here and living
with Zachary Grant, I thought I'd see your cheeks
glowing with happiness."

"We've got a few things to work out."

Beth leaned forward slightly. "You want to talk
about it?"

Amanda shook her head. Much as she'd like to
confide in her friend—to confide in *someone*—she
wasn't going to talk about Zachary's problem. It was
too personal.

"Is he being good to you?" Beth probed.

"Very good."

"Then what's the problem?"

"Nothing serious."

"When I first met him, I thought he was perfect for you. Am I going to be disappointed?"

"No!" she answered, because she was going to make this work—if the cure killed them both.

"Okay. Let's go out to lunch to celebrate the first new Esther Scott column."

"You haven't even read it yet."

"Actually I have."

Amanda blinked. "How? I just put it on your desk a few minutes ago."

"After you left the house, I phoned Zach and told him you'd called and said you left it home, and you wanted him to e-mail it."

"That's kind of sneaky, don't you think."

Beth had the grace to look embarrassed before she began talking rapidly. "Point taken. But I knew your material was going to be great. I wanted to be able to tell you that today, because I know you're a perfectionist. Besides, I know you were agonizing over getting it right. Well, you have nothing to worry about. In my professional opinion, it's wonderful. Just what our readers are looking for. You're better than Esther Knight ever was. You're more sensitive to the needs of the readers. You're a better writer. And you're more in tune with today's young women."

Amanda flushed with pleasure. "I…I don't know what to say."

"Accept the praise graciously. Then get started on your next installment."

"I've been looking at letters, deciding which ones I want to answer."

"Good. Let's go to lunch, then. I've made reservations at a little Italian restaurant I discovered. If we leave now, we can beat the noontime crowd."

"Italian sounds fine," Amanda answered, thinking that she'd been eating far too much good food lately. Both she and Zach had been doing a lot of cooking— as a way to take their minds off sex.

Sex. Every thought she had led back to sex.

"Earth to Amanda." Beth broke in to her musings.

"Sorry."

"You're thinking about jumping Zach's bones, aren't you?"

"Yes," Amanda answered, although she knew Beth didn't understand the import of her question.

"Well, try to keep your mind on business for a while. Because over lunch, I want to discuss some ideas with you."

"Like what?"

"Like writing some articles for *Vanessa* under your own name."

"Oh my. What did you have in mind?"

"What would you think about a piece on controlling men? Hmm—I mean men who need to control their women."

Amanda swallowed. "I guess Tony Anderson made you think about that?"

"Uh-huh."

Actually, she'd already started contemplating writing about the subject—as a way of exorcising her own ghosts. "Yes, I'd like that," she answered.

"Good. And I have some other ideas we can discuss over wood-fired pizzas. Or white bean and tuna salad."

"Sounds good."

In fact, lunch was delicious—and productive. Beth gave her several more article ideas, and she left the meeting thinking that she might actually be able to make a living from her writing. Certainly her name on articles in *Vanessa* would make it easier to sell her book. And maybe she could write for other publications—if that was okay with Beth.

She was on her way back to New Jersey before rush-hour traffic could bog her down.

Pulling up at the curb, she stopped to admire Zach's house. She'd been afraid he'd pick something new and modern, but he'd bought a thirties bungalow with a wide front porch and a roof held up by real stone columns. The neighborhood was old and settled, with large trees, quiet streets and big backyards.

Inside, Zach had done a lot of work. He'd remodeled and enlarged the kitchen. And he'd refinished all the beautiful woodwork and hardwood floors.

It was a house where she'd love to live. A house where she'd love to raise children. But both of them had been careful not to talk about the future. She suspected that Zach wasn't going to do that until he resolved the problem that had been hanging over him for a year.

And no amount of talking about it was going to make him feel okay. He had to see for himself that they could make love like any other couple.

Actually, she'd done a lot of research about his condition since he'd told her what was wrong. The chapters of books and articles she'd read recommended exercises to help a dysfunctional couple get in touch with each other physically. Starting with touching and kissing. Giving back rubs and massages. Physical closeness with no pressure to progress to intercourse.

The concept was sound, but she honestly didn't think either one of them could go that route. Not right now. She wanted Zach too much, and he wanted her. And if they got into anything explicit, they'd end up in bed. And it might not work out.

She wasn't all that worried about "failure." She knew it might take time for Zach to get back to what most people would consider normal. But she was pretty sure he'd be upset if they tried intercourse and he didn't have an orgasm.

So she was still holding off any sexual contact—although it was getting more difficult each day. Each hour. Each minute. She was starting to think of alternatives. What about manual stimulation? Could she bring him to climax with her hand—with her mouth? Perhaps they could start with that.

She was making herself hot just thinking about it. And his car was in the driveway. So she knew he wasn't down at the office that he rented in a small office building a couple of miles away.

He was inside. Waiting for her. And she had to sit in the car for a while, getting her breathing back to normal before she entered the house.

When she walked into the kitchen, Zach was standing in front of the stove, stirring a large pot of soup.

He looked up, and she could tell immediately how glad he was to see her. She wanted to tell him she could come home to that look on his face for the next hundred years, but she didn't want to make him feel any more pressure than he already did.

She settled for, "Hi. I'm glad to be back. I always forget how much I hate the city."

"Hi, yourself."

"What's that?" she asked, gesturing toward the soup.

"Oxtail soup."

She peered into the pot. "You're kidding. Isn't that something from the Middle Ages?"

"Maybe that's where it originated. But it's a recipe I've been using for years. It's really good. The oxtails give it a wonderful flavor and a nice, thick texture. And there are all kinds of chunky vegetables."

"Well, you're a better cook than I am," she answered.

"I've made a lot of stuff out of books." Turning from the pot, he asked, "How did the meeting go?"

Unable to keep the excitement out of her voice, she answered, "Beth wants me to do some other articles for her."

"That's great. I know you've got to be pleased." Zach stepped away from the stove and reached to hug her. She went into his arms, then caught her breath as she catalogued the instant reaction of his body—and her own.

She felt her breathing accelerate, felt her heart pounding against the wall of her chest.

He dipped his head, brushing aside her hair with his nose and planting little kisses on her neck. Little kisses that fanned the flames. They were two people who cared about each other—so much. Yet they couldn't be easy with each other. Not yet.

"Oh Lord, Amanda, I'm going crazy with wanting you," he growled.

She stayed in his arms another few seconds, then pushed gently against his shoulders, and he let her go. "We're both going crazy," she said in a husky voice. "That's the idea."

"When is enough enough?" he asked.

"Let's see if we can hold out for a week."

He groaned.

Sitting down at the kitchen table, she searched around for a neutral topic. As soon as she spoke, she realized that nothing she could say was really neutral. "You were out of the house so late last night. What were you doing—going for a five-mile jog?"

"Actually, I was doing an insurance investigation. There's a guy who claims to be disabled from a fall down the stairs. And he's trying to collect big time on his disability insurance. I snapped some pictures of him lifting heavy garbage cans and taking them out to the curb."

"Clever!"

"Yeah, that should screw up his case."

"How did you know when to take the pictures?"

"I found out his trash day. And then I established that his garbage cans were always at the curb the night before."

She laughed. "I guess you have to be creative to be a private detective."

"Yes," he said, his voice husky, and she knew that he was thinking about other times he'd been creative—like when he'd turned her bedroom into a love nest.

She shifted in her seat. He went back to tending the soup, but she saw that his hand was clenched around the handle of the big spoon.

After several minutes of silence, they started talking about his work again. She didn't say much about hers. She couldn't, because that would mean talking about sex—or talking about Tony Anderson. And both of those topics were off-limits—for two different reasons.

So she chatted with him for a few more minutes,

then said she needed to take some notes on her conversation with Beth.

Upstairs, after taking off the skirt and jacket she'd worn into town, she changed into jeans and a T-shirt, then tried to get some work done. When she came back again, Zach, who was chopping vegetables for a salad, looked up as she entered the room.

"I was thinking that biscuits would taste good with that soup" she said.

"You bet."

"Do you have the makings?"

"I think so. You can check the pantry and the refrigerator."

She found flour, butter, milk, baking powder and salt. She'd made a lot of biscuits over the years. Mom had been a biscuit expert, and she'd made sure her daughters acquired that skill. So Beth was able to guess at the proportions, then add a little more milk when the mix was a tad dry.

She tried to stay out of Zach's way, but as she moved around the kitchen, she was very aware of exactly where he was and what he was doing. And from the way he quickly drew back when she approached the sink, she guessed he was also in a state of high alert. When she reached to turn on the oven, her breast brushed against his arm, and they both drew in a sharp breath.

He said nothing, only turned to give her a penetrating look.

"Are drop biscuits okay? Or should I roll them out?"

"Do it the easy way."

"That's what I was hoping you'd say."

She made quick work of getting small mounds of

dough onto a baking sheet, then began setting the table.

As they sat across from each other, he buttered one of her biscuits and took a bite. "This is good."

"Thanks." She spooned up some soup. "I didn't know if I'd like this, but it's delicious."

"Basically, it's beef and vegetables with a fancy name."

"Right."

He shifted in his seat. "I like sharing meals with you."

"Yes. I like it, too. And we work well together."

The conversation ground to a halt again, and they each focused on their food.

Lord, if she couldn't do any better than this, she was in trouble, she thought.

They used up the last of the milk in her after-dinner coffee. As she turned from throwing the empty container into the trash can, she found him staring at her.

"What?"

"You look so kissable."

Unconsciously, she flicked her tongue over her lower lip.

"Very kissable."

"Zach…"

He was standing with his palms pressed against his hips, as if to keep from reaching for her. "Are you really going to keep up this torture for the rest of the week?" he asked, and she caught the undercurrent of frustration in his voice.

"We…should," she answered, knowing that she didn't sound entirely sure anymore.

He stood looking at her for several minutes. "Um, maybe I'd better get out of here and try to cool off.

I'll go to the grocery store and buy some milk. Then I'll stop at the video store and pick up some DVDs. I'll be gone for a couple of hours. Okay?''

''Yes. That's a good idea,'' she managed to say when she wanted to reach for him, to hold him close. He'd be hard. And she imagined pressing her middle against his erection. He was taller than she. But if he leaned back against the counter the way he'd leaned against the door that time, then he'd be right where she wanted him.

The vivid picture in her mind sent heat shooting through her.

''Go on,'' she said.

He turned and walked out of the kitchen.

Was Dr. O'Neal's prescription too draconian? *Was* she driving them both insane? She felt on the edge of madness. She'd never been so sexually frustrated in her life. Yet she didn't want to ruin things for Zach. If he tried to make love to her and couldn't climax, he was going to feel worse than he had the last time. And waiting a few more days might make the difference for him.

Or would it?

Maybe they'd both had enough. Maybe it was time for something different.

Quickly she picked up the phone and dialed information. After getting the number she wanted, she made a call.

It took only a few minutes to make some strategic arrangements. Then she hurried to her computer and started writing a letter.

17

ZACH HAD TAKEN his time at the video store, but he knew the moment he walked in the door that the house was empty.

Amanda usually called out to him when he came home. But she didn't do that now. And he realized he hadn't seen her car outside.

His stomach clenched. She'd gone. He guessed she'd had enough of the tension zapping back and forth between them, and she'd left him. Well, he couldn't blame her.

On wooden legs, he carried the carton of milk to the kitchen—where he saw a piece of paper sitting in the middle of the table. His heart started pounding as he regarded the letter lying there, catching the light and reflecting it back to him.

Snatching it up, he read rapidly.

Dear Esther,
I don't know what to do. My boyfriend and I are driving each other around the bend. Some crazy sex therapist told her that our sex life would be a whole lot better if we didn't touch each other for a week. We followed the therapist's advice. Now both of us are so hot it's like sparks hitting dry tinder. What do you suggest we do about it?

Burning up in Paramus.

He couldn't help grinning. Burning up in Paramus was a pretty good description of the way he felt.

But there was more on the paper. An answer, apparently.

Dear Paramus,
If you're burning up the house, then both of you need a change of scenery. So treat him to a night out. Why not rent a fancy hotel room, and see if you can make some changes in the way you're dealing with each other?

Esther Scott

Below the letters was an address and room number. Of a *very* fancy, very pricey hotel. The Eden Palace.

He reread the letter and the answer. Read them again. Then he walked back to the car and started driving to the Eden Palace.

THE KNOCK ON THE DOOR made Amanda jump. She'd been sitting in the large room, waiting for Zach, hoping he'd come. At first she'd been busy getting ready. Turning down lights. Getting out candles. Making sure the champagne was chilled. Changing into the outfit she'd decided to wear. Then there had been nothing to do but wait and think about how important the next few hours would be. Before she'd met Zachary Grant, she'd been reasonably happy with her life—if you forgot about the nasty little episode at Harmons College. But Zach had made her realize that she was only existing, not living. She'd always thought she'd get married some day and settle down. Now she knew how much she'd been missing while she focused on her career. And how much she desperately wanted to make her relationship with Zach into something permanent.

"Who's there?" she called in a quavery voice.

"Burning up in Paramus," he answered, sounding about as nervous as she felt.

Maybe that was good. Maybe it wasn't.

"That was my line," she said as she turned the knob and stepped aside. He hurried into the room and closed the door. But once they were alone, they stood in the middle of the large space, looking nervously at each other.

She saw him swallow as he stared around the opulent bedroom, taking in the Queen Anne furniture, the velvet drapes, the thick carpeting, the wide, four-poster bed with what looked like a silk coverlet. "What is this, the honeymoon suite?" he asked in a thick voice.

She lifted her chin and gave him a "make something of it" look. "As a matter of fact it is."

She watched his eyes sweep over her. "No silk nightgown to go with the theme?"

"Not tonight," she murmured. Actually, she'd dressed carefully for the evening in a loose shift that covered her from her neck to midcalf, along with high-heeled sandals. What looked like a rather demure outfit, if she did say so herself.

To change the subject she said, "How about some champagne?" Without waiting for an answer, she walked to the bucket sitting on a tray beside the bed.

When she fumbled to get the cork out, he came up behind her and took the bottle from her hand. Then he opened it and poured them both a glass. But she could see that his hands weren't a lot steadier than hers.

She took a quick swallow and saw he had done the same. So much for iron nerves. Hers and his.

He didn't speak, and she knew she was the one who would need to do the talking. Gulping in air, she said, "When I invited myself to stay in your house, I...I thought I was doing the right thing...for both of us. But maybe I was wrong."

"And maybe you're right," he answered quickly. "Because God knows, I've wanted you with me." He swallowed. "Even if I've been a little... uh...grumpy."

"I'm glad—I mean glad that you wanted me there."

The warm look on his face made her want to cross the space that separated them and take him in her arms. But she stayed where she was because she knew that they needed to do things differently. If they fell back into the same old pattern, they could get into trouble again.

"Before you went out tonight, I was thinking about Dr. O'Neal's prescription. I was thinking that maybe we could try a slightly different approach," she said, then hurried on. "I mean we know that you haven't been able to have an orgasm during intercourse. But what if we took an intermediate step?"

When he stared inquiringly at her, she went on, "Suppose I bring you to climax some other way?"

"Why do you think that will work?" he asked quietly.

She had come up with the answer when she'd first thought of renting this room. "For one thing, because I'll be doing it for my own pleasure."

He was listening intently, which gave her the resolve to continue. "You won't have to worry about…about performing, because I'll be the one in charge. I'll be doing what I want to do.''

"We tried that once before. It didn't work out the way you expected," he said.

"That was then. This is now. This time I've got something completely different in mind."

His doubtful look made her desperate to convince him that her new plan would work. After setting down her glass, she crossed the room and took his glass from his hand. Then she slid her arms around him.

"Oh Lord, Amanda, you don't know how much I've wanted to hug you tight. Just hug you and hang on," he breathed.

"I know. Believe me, I do."

When he clasped her body to his, she let out a small sigh as she closed her eyes and pressed her head to his shoulder, breathing in his masculine scent.

His erection was like an exclamation point between them. "Amanda, I don't want to disappoint you," he said in a barely audible voice. "That's why I've been playing by your rules. That's the only reason I've been able to keep from dragging you to bed. Because I knew it could turn out just the way it always does for me. And I know you want…you want…"

Before he could finish, she interrupted him. "Oh, Zach. You won't disappoint me," she answered, kissing his shoulder through the fabric of his T-shirt. "Not this time. I'm going to make sure that doesn't happen. All you have to do is enjoy my fantasy."

His greedy hands slid up and down her back, then stopped abruptly. "Lord, you're not wearing a bra under that dress!" he growled.

She raised her head and gave him a sweet look.

"Actually, I'm not wearing *anything* under this dress."

He swore, then set her away from him. "I suppose you know what that piece of information is doing to me?"

She met his eyes with a steady gaze. "To me, too. Every time I move, I feel the fabric move against my breasts."

He made a strangled exclamation.

"Actually, I've had the past hour and a half to turn myself on thinking about your meeting me here. But it's not just the turn-on. It's more than that. Our relationship is important to me, and I want it to work out," she said, revealing as much as she dared.

"So do I!"

"Then let me have my wicked way with you."

He arched an inquiring eyebrow.

Trying to sound bold, she raised her chin and said. "Let me set up another little game for us to play. Where I'm in total charge of your body."

He tipped his head to one side, as he considered the implications. "As in...uh...bondage?"

"Well...honorary bondage."

"What...uh...does that mean?"

She stiffened her posture and made her voice authoritative. "It means I want you naked on your back on that bed. With your arms spread-eagle. And I expect you to stay that way, until I say you can move."

She finished by marching past him to the bed and yanking the silk coverlet and top sheet off the end, so that only the bottom sheet remained.

Whirling back to him, she ordered, "Now take off your clothes, and lie down."

With her breath frozen in her lungs, she waited to see what would happen.

When Zach started to pull his T-shirt over his head, she let the captive breath trickle out.

He turned away from her, and when he tossed his shirt onto the chair, she admired the taut muscles of his broad back and nicely shaped arms. When he shucked off his jeans and briefs, she looked at his very masculine butt with appreciation. But she kept her voice hard and commanding in keeping with the role she had set herself to play.

"Lie down."

He hesitated a moment, then did as she asked, and she saw what she had only felt earlier—his cock was taut with arousal.

"Well, you're hard as a fencepost. I see I'll have something to work with," she said in a conversational tone.

Ignoring his strangled exclamation, she moved toward the edge of the bed and looked down at him. "Put your arms out to the sides. The way I told you I wanted them."

He did, but not to their full extension, as though he was afraid to trust her all the way.

"Farther," she ordered, and he slowly did her bidding until he looked like a sacrificial victim.

His eyes were wary. "What are you going to do?" he asked in a taut voice.

"Hmm, perhaps you should have an honorary gag over your mouth, too. I don't plan to explain myself. And I don't want you to speak unless I give you permission."

He gave her a doubtful look but pressed his lips together.

"Nice. Very nice," she murmured. "Do you know, you are so sexy like that? And so vulnerable. And you'll just have to wait to see what I have in mind. But first I think we need a little more light so we can both enjoy what I'm doing."

He started to speak again, but she gave him a stern look, and he firmed his lips once more. Walking to the desk, she turned on that one lamp, then returned to the bed. Looking down at him, she said, "Remember I told you how important it is for a man and a woman to communicate what works for each of them." Smiling, she added, "It's convenient that you let me know what you like to look at." As she spoke, she reached to the placket at the front of her dress and began opening the buttons. She knew his gaze was glued to her busy fingers. When she had opened the bodice just above her waist, she pushed the fabric out of the way on either side, exposing her breasts with their tight, aroused tips. Arching her back, she lifted the mounds in her hands, then stroked them, hearing Zach make a muffled moan as he watched.

Smiling again, she circled her taut nipples with her fingers, then squeezed and tugged at them, watching the hungry expression on his face.

"Mmm, that feels so exciting," she whispered, thinking that it was a good thing she couldn't reach orgasm just from breast stimulation.

She stood there for another few moments, torturing herself and Zach. When she eased onto the bed, she heard him draw in a strangled breath.

"I think I know what you'd like me to do, but you're going to have to wait for that," she purred as she stroked her fingers over his shoulders, then combed her fingers through the hair on his chest before finding his nipples and doing what she had done to herself, wringing a gasp from him.

Before he could enjoy that too much, she glided her hand lower, over his ribs, then his abdomen. His muscles jumped under her fingers. And when she by-passed his cock and ran her nails up one thigh, he made a pleading sound.

She went up on her knees then, pulling the dress up to her waist, showing him that she was naked underneath, as promised.

Gathering the skirt up with one hand, she used the other to play with the blond hair at the juncture of her legs, then slid her hand a little lower. But she stayed away from her clit because she was too close to the edge to risk touching herself there.

Lifting one shoulder, she said sweetly, "You know, all this fabric is in the way." Then, slowly, tantalizingly slowly, she eased her arms out of the sleeves, pulled the dress over her head and tossed it onto the floor.

"Lord, this is making me so hot," she said, arching her back, lifting her hair off her shoulders and letting it fall back, knowing his gaze was following every move she made. Knowing she was probably driving him mad—because she knew what she was doing to herself.

When she reached out and delicately glided one finger along the length of his red, swollen cock, she saw his hands grab at the sheet. She couldn't meet his gaze then. Because if she did, she'd let herself give in to the pleading look in his eyes and the harsh sound of his breathing.

Instead she continued with the teasing stroking of one finger, before taking him delicately in her fist, moving up and down the shaft in a way she was pretty sure would drive him toward completion.

And her, too. Because she didn't know how much more of this she could take. Teasing him, touching him like this was almost more than she could stand.

Leaning over, she stroked him with her tongue, hearing his strangled exclamation. From the corner of her eye, she saw his hands twist at the sheet. When she took him into her mouth, he made a low animal sound.

Using her lips and tongue, she pushed him further—pushed him toward the point of no return. And she knew she had him close to the edge. She could feel him trembling. Feel him straining not to lift his hips off the mattress as she pleasured him.

All the signs were there. He was close to orgasm. And when she knew he was poised on the fine edge of release, she suddenly changed the rules—straddling him so that she could bring his rock-hard erection inside her.

She raised her head then, saw his look of shock as she began to move.

Seconds later, he came, his shout of triumph rocketing through the room. She was almost as far gone as he. Leaning forward, she pressed her clit against him, moving frantically until she followed him over the edge, her own triumph soaring through her.

She hadn't given him permission to move. But he gathered her to him, pulling her down so that she was sprawled on top of him as he kissed her and stroked his hands over her back and hips.

"Amanda, oh Lord, Amanda," he whispered. "Thank you. Thank you so much."

She kissed his cheek. "Thank you for trusting me."

Closing her eyes, she drifted on a warm wave of contentment as he clasped her to him.

When she felt a chuckle rumble in his chest, she raised her head and looked at him inquiringly.

"Very clever of you, you little witch."

"I thought that naughty little game might be the right way to go. Something entirely different."

"Yeah. And not telling me what you had planned for the grand finale." He continued to caress her, then turned and nibbled his lips against her cheek before reaching to switch on one of the bedside lights.

When their eyes had adjusted, he smoothed back a lock of blond hair that had fallen across her forehead.

The intensity of his eyes told her he wanted to say something important, and her breath caught.

"Amanda, I love you. I feel like I've been waiting to say that for a hundred years. But I think you know why I couldn't do it. Not until I fixed my problem. Or—you fixed it, actually."

"Oh, Zach, I love you. I felt like I had to wait to say it, too."

"So now that that's settled, how would you feel about marrying me?" he asked in a voice barely above a whisper.

She leaned closer and kissed the dark stubble along his jawline. "I was hoping you'd ask."

He let out a long, relieved sigh. "I wanted to. You don't know how much I wanted to."

She found his hand and knit her fingers with his.

"I'm glad you thought of coming here," he murmured.

She laughed. "Both of us came, actually."

"Yeah." He stayed beside her for several moments longer, then eased away so that he could walk to the end of the bed and retrieve the covers. When they were back in place, he picked up the glasses of champagne. After she sat up, he handed her a glass and climbed back into bed.

"To us," he whispered.

"Yes, to us."

They both took a sip.

"I can taste it now," she murmured.

He laughed. "Yeah. Before, it might as well have been vinegar."

He took another sip, then set down the glass and turned his head, nibbling his lips against her cheek, her ear. "Loving you makes all the difference," he murmured. "I think that's why your bondage game worked."

"Oh, Zach. Maybe that is true."

He clasped her tightly, then drew back again. "I'm not trying to push you. But how soon do you think we can get married?"

"As soon as we can get a license."

"You don't want a big fancy wedding?"

"Not if we have to make a bunch of arrangements. I just want Beth—and a couple of my old friends from Harmons. People who stuck by me. And my sister."

"My family will fill up the room."

"I don't mind. Whatever you want."

His expression changed, and she knew he was thinking of something serious.

"What?"

"Uh…before we get too carried away, do you remember that talk we had at the restaurant? Where I said I'd like to go back to the police force. How would you feel about that?'' he asked.

He was sitting very still, waiting for her answer.

"I'd feel fine about it. I told you."

"That was hypothetical. This is for real."

"Zach, you and I are for real. It's a real relationship. It's going to be a real marriage. Where we each give and take so we can each be happy."

He kissed her hair, her cheek. "The luckiest day of my life was the day I rang your doorbell."

"And embarrassed the heck out of me. You know what I was doing—right?"

He laughed. "Well, I didn't know for sure, until now."

"Writing the column turned me on. I guess that's an occupational hazard."

"I don't think you're going to need that vibrator anymore."

"I already tossed it in the trash, before I came up here."

He looked over at her. "You were certain things were going to work out?"

"I wanted them to. So much. That's why I had to come here tonight and play out that scenario." She swallowed. "You know it was hard for me to do all that."

"I could tell."

"Uh-huh."

"You'll never make a dominatrix. You were too adorable."

"I'll show you adorable." She raised her fist, but he grabbed her arm and brought it back under the covers. "Don't tell me you weren't...apprehensive," she demanded.

"Okay. I was worried."

"Good. You were supposed to be."

"The point is, I liked it. And it worked."

She swallowed. "Yes." Then, because she was determined to be honest, she added, "You introduced me to facets of my sexuality that I would never have discovered on my own. If you hadn't showed me there were all kinds of inventive ways to make love, I never could have pulled off that act a few minutes ago."

"Right. I was inventive because I was desperate to make love with you—any way I could."

"Any way. All ways," she answered. "But I'm glad we solved your problem. Because I know it was bothering you. And it would have kept eating at you—even if I kept assuring you that it didn't matter."

"So you devised a week of torture for us both."

"I figured that the hornier we got, the more chance we had of success. Only we didn't make it through a week."

"Horny. That's a nice, scientific way to put it, Dr. O'Neal."

"I'm rather proud of my deductive reasoning skills."

They grinned at each other. She hadn't felt this good in years.

"Well, I think that we'd better test your hypothesis, to make sure it's not a one-time deal."

"I'm sure it's not."

"Good. Because we're going to have a little role reversal."

"What do you mean?" she asked, afraid she already knew the answer.

"This time, you're the one who gets chained to the bed. Honorary chains of course. Lie down and put your hands out to the sides, and don't move them unless I give you permission. And maybe for this round, you'll wear an honorary blindfold, too."

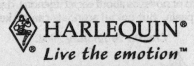

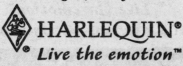

If you enjoyed what you just read,
then we've got an offer you can't resist!

Take 2 bestselling
love stories FREE!

Plus get a FREE surprise gift!

///////////////////

Clip this page and mail it to Harlequin Reader Service®

IN U.S.A.	IN CANADA
3010 Walden Ave.	P.O. Box 609
P.O. Box 1867	Fort Erie, Ontario
Buffalo, N.Y. 14240-1867	L2A 5X3

YES! Please send me 2 free Blaze™ novels and my free surprise gift. After
receiving them, if I don't wish to receive anymore, I can return the shipping
statement marked cancel. If I don't cancel, I will receive 4 brand-new novels
each month, before they're available in stores! In the U.S.A., bill me at the
bargain price of $3.80 plus 25¢ shipping and handling per book and applicable
sales tax, if any*. In Canada, bill me at the bargain price of $4.21 plus 25¢
shipping and handling per book and applicable taxes**. That's the complete
price and a savings of at least 10% off the cover prices—what a great deal! I
understand that accepting the 2 free books and gift places me under no
obligation ever to buy any books. I can always return a shipment and cancel at
any time. Even if I never buy another book from Harlequin, the 2 free books and
gift are mine to keep forever.

150 HDN DNWD
350 HDN DNWE

Name	(PLEASE PRINT)	
Address	Apt.#	
City	State/Prov.	Zip/Postal Code

* Terms and prices subject to change without notice. Sales tax applicable in N.Y.
** Canadian residents will be charged applicable provincial taxes and GST.
   All orders subject to approval. Offer limited to one per household and not valid to
   current Blaze™ subscribers.
® are registered trademarks of Harlequin Enterprises Limited.

BLZ02-R

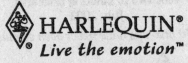

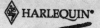